MELT

Diana Rock

Enjoy the Read!
Diana Rock

Melt My Heart

Fulton River Falls, Volume 1

Diana Rock

Published by Diana Rock, 2021.

MELT MY HEART

Copyright © 2021 by Denise M. Long
All Rights reserved.

No part of this book may be used or reproduced in any manner whatsoever including audio recording without written permission of the author and Copyright holder. This author supports the right to free expression and values copyright protection. The scanning, uploading, and distribution of this book in any manner or medium without permission of the copyright holder is theft of the property. Thank you for supporting this author's creative work with your purchase.

Print IBSN: 978-1-7360371-1-9

Digital IBSN: 978-1-7360371-0-2

Editor: Lynne Pearson, Allthatediting.com

This is a work of fiction. Names, characters, places, and incidents either are the product of the author's imagination or are used fictitiously, and any resemblance to actual persons, living or dead, business establishments, organizations, events, locale, or weather events is entirely coincidental.

Dedication

This book is dedicated to Nancy.

Thank you, Sweetheart, for reminding me that life is finite and to get on with my dreams. Love and miss you forever.

CHAPTER ONE

Tired but not wanting to go home yet after another long day at work, Jamaica Jones wandered over to O'Toole's Tavern. She blinked several times before she could make out the tavern's interior. Dark red, vinyl-covered booths lined the walls on three sides, the fourth side holding the wooden bar. Patrick O'Toole stood behind the bar, like a stereotypical bartender, wiping pilsner glasses dry before placing them on the sideboard.

Jamaica took a seat at the end of the bar.

"Cosmo, please, Pat," she said when he walked over to wait on her.

"Coming up, sweetie." He grabbed the shaker. "How's your father doing these days?"

"Fairly well. Between me, the visiting nurses, and the home health aides, we manage to keep him out of trouble." Jamaica watched as the man poured vodka, triple sec, cranberry juice, and lime juice into the shaker, added a few ice cubes, then flipped a glass over the top. He shook it vigorously before pouring the contents into a martini glass. With a flourish, he dropped a twist of lime rind on the rim.

Patrick set the glass of frothy pink liquid in front of Jamaica. "Let it settle a few seconds. I shook it pretty hard."

Jamaica didn't wait. Gingerly taking the glass, she sipped the first inch of liquor from it, and closed her eyes. *Ah, beautiful! Pat still knows how to make a great cosmo. He probably doesn't receive many requests for one in Fulton River.* The sweet and tart tastes lingered on her tongue pleasantly.

The chink of a cue hitting a ball came from the pool table in the back corner of the room. Clustered around the pool table were four men. Three of the men, Jamaica recognized from high school – Isaac Young, John Hampton, and Eric Shultz. The back of the fourth man looked familiar. Jamaica's gut clenched even though she couldn't see his face.

He turned around.

No. No, please don't be Ronnie. Her gut clenched harder. She tried not to stare, tried to take another sip of her drink but the glass stayed suspended in midair, waiting for a brain signal to bring it to her lips.

The fourth man gestured toward her while speaking with the other three guys, set his cue down, then broke off from them and approached her.

Jamaica couldn't move. It had been so long. Somehow, he looked nearly the same — the same sandy-blond hair, and the same blue-green eyes. Same scar just above his left eyebrow. There was no mistaking Ronald Caswell.

"Hey, Jam. How are you?" he asked, settling onto the seat beside her.

Finally, *finally*, she put the glass down and tried her best to smile. "Hey Ronnie. Welcome home."

"Thanks. It's been a long time," he boldly looked her over.

Jamaica fingered the stem of her martini glass. "Yes, it has. Twelve years. How's the police business?"

"Done. I'm out." He signaled to Patrick for a beer.

"After what — ten years?"

"Eleven. I'm back home to stay now." He looked down at his legs.

"Good for you. Put in your time and you're out. That's great." She sipped her cosmo.

Patrick placed the bottle in front of Ronnie and walked away.

Ronnie's Adam's apple bobbed, and he cleared his throat. "God, it's great to see you again."

Jamaica's cheeks blushed warm. She cast her eyes down. He was still as handsome, maybe more so now, than he was the last time she had seen him at high school graduation. Raising her eyes, she glanced at his ring finger — still bare. A surge of electricity zipped along her spine. Not only had he been her first love, he'd been her only real love. Now here he was, gorgeous and still single. *Could he possibly?* Jamaica shook her head. *Not that I would even consider it after what happened.*

"It's great to see you again too. It's been a long time," she said, then realized she had repeated him. Heat spread throughout her face. *Duh!*

Whistles from the other three guys made Ronnie look over toward the pool table. They wanted their fourth player back.

"I'll call you."

"Sure. It would be good to catch up," she replied, already turning back toward the bar. "I'm usually at the Emporium. You can call me there."

"The Ice Cream Emporium? You work for Mr. Nichol?" Ronnie asked, getting up off the bar stool and grabbing his beer bottle.

"I own it now. Stop by sometime. Come see what I did to the shop." She smiled at him, her head held high.

Ronnie's smile dropped amid a background of harassment from his pool buddies echoing across the tavern. He backed away faster now. "I'll see ya."

***

For Ronnie, seeing Jamaica Jones again was bittersweet and, as it turned out, a curse. When he moved back to town and considered opening his new store, it was with a niggling hope that he'd see Jamaica again. And here she was, all grown up into a beautiful, full-figured woman. She might have even grown a couple inches taller since the last time he'd seen her.

His mind tallied through all the dates and relationships he'd had over the years since high school. They had been sporadic and usually short-lived. Even so, he never got over Jamaica's amber brown eyes and sharp wit. The memory of those eyes seemed to soften the hard chip on his shoulder every time he thought of them. And he had thought of them a lot over the years.

Hearing she owned old Mr. Nichol's Ice Cream Emporium was not good news. It was probably the worst news he could have heard from her. He'd have rather heard she was married with six kids and pregnant with numbers seven and eight.

It was too late now. He'd signed the lease. He'd bought the equipment. It was already being delivered. Supplies he'd purchased were due any day now. And the candy and ice cream he would be selling was on order — on hold for delivery until he finished refurbishing the store's interior. Grandma and Grandpa Caswell's old confections shop was going to be back in business.

Ronnie placed his beer on the side table and reached for his pool cue.

He didn't want to see the look on Jamaica's face when she realized he would be in direct competition with her shop. It was bad enough to be in competition with someone you knew, but to have it happen with someone you have history — strong history with, was entirely different. He rubbed his left thigh as he studied the pool table spread. The urge to flee, to be anywhere but here, surged through his bones.

"Come on, Caswell, shoot for God's sake." Eric slurred over the lip of his beer bottle.

Perhaps he should tell her outright before she found out. That might be the best course of action. Truth was, he was too chicken to do it. Somehow his tongue twisted up into tangles when he spoke with her, and to do so about such a subject might be the death of him. She wouldn't believe him anyway. No, he couldn't talk to her about it, couldn't warn her of his plans. She was going to have to find out the hard way and hate him even more for it. Because this time, he intended to put the Emporium out of business as payback for bankrupting his grandparents' business. And to save his own.

***

MELT MY HEART

Jamaica Jones' butt wasn't in the chair two seconds before the bell on the front door tinkled again. Amber brown eyes rolling to heaven, she palm-slapped both hands on her desk, hefting herself to her feet and strode out to the front of the ice cream shop to wait on her customers. She chastised herself for being peeved about these patrons. They were what kept the store going financially and she needed every single one who walked through that door. Even so, she couldn't help wishing, just once, she could finish her accounting statements and bookkeeping during business hours rather than have to work on them at home.

She walked through the white lattice and spindle framed archway into her ice cream parlor. Striding the length of the aisle behind the marble-topped counter, she glanced to her right to check her reflection in the hipped mirrors ringed with white lights on the wall behind the shelves of jars. Forty different jars holding everything from different types of nuts and seeds, four different types of sprinkles, and fourteen varieties of crushed cookies and candy pieces.

"Hey Jam, how's it going today?" said a tall, wiry man with hair as orange as a carrot.

"Hey Kevin. Busy day. How about yourself?"

"Card shop's been pretty quiet this week. Third week in a row." He peered up at the list of thirty ice cream flavors available. Slowly, he walked the length of the white-paneled and marble-topped counter, one hand resting on the end of his chin, the index finger tapping his mouth. Once reaching the end of the counter, he turned, and came back to the beginning.

Jamaica waited patiently behind the counter, tying on her frilled Victorian style apron to keep her long red skirt and short-sleeved, white linen blouse clean. "Let's see, today I'll take two scoops of banana marshmallow on a sugar cone."

"You got it." Turning to face the two, ten-foot-long freezer cases of ice cream lining the wall below the shelves of jars, she picked up the nearest ice cream scoop and reached for a sugar cone.

She carefully scooped the sweet ice cream into, and on top of the fragile cone. As she tamped the scoops down lightly to prevent them from falling off, Jamaica spoke over her shoulder, "How's that lovely wife of yours and those adorable children?"

"Oh, they're doing fine. Sara lost her two front teeth this weekend. Looks cute as a bug. Zachary's in trouble at school for stealing someone's pencil." Kevin leaned against the counter with one hand while his other hand fished his wallet out of his back pocket.

Jamaica turned back toward him and smiled as she presented the cone and a napkin to Kevin Dailey, in exchange for his five-dollar bill. "Enjoy." She rang up the sale on the massive, Victorian era register, and tucked the bill into the cash drawer. After it clicked shut, she leaned forward against the counter to politely watch her latest customer leave.

"You bet." Kevin walked to the front door and opened it. Before stepping outside, he halted in his tracks. "Whoa, will you look at that!" He stood transfixed in the open doorway, staring at something diagonally across the street.

"What is it?" Jamaica walked around the counter and joined Kevin at the door.

He didn't answer, his mouth and tongue busy trying to keep up with the dripping ice cream in the Vermont June heat. They both stood rooted in the doorway watching as a huge truck-mounted crane swung a massive crate from the back of a flatbed truck onto the sidewalk outside a vacant storefront.

"Wonder what's going on, that storefront's been empty for ages." Kevin stared at the workmen, mesmerized. Then realizing his ice cream cone was dripping banana marshmallow down his fingers onto the floor, he rapidly licked all around the bulging, slippery mess. Stooping, he wiped up the drips on the polished black and white checkered tile floor with his napkin. Standing again, he resumed licking the melting mass of sugar and cream.

MELT MY HEART

"Looks like we finally have a new neighbor." Jamaica watched as the crew of four men set the crate down on the sidewalk and untied it from the crane. Her eyes swerved over to the store's front windows. The large panes of glass were lined with paper from the inside. *Had they always been like that? Wasn't there a "FOR LEASE/RENT" sign there yesterday?*

Kevin walked through the open door, stopping again to face Jamaica. "Looks like it. Let me see what I can find out. I'll let you know." And Kevin walked into his card and gift store next door.

Curiosity kept Jamaica riveted to the spot in her doorway, her hands fidgeting with her apron, staring, as the four men struggled to uncrate a commercial refrigerator then carry it into the building.

Much like her own building and every other building on Main Street, it was made of aged red brick, having been built in the early 1900s. The street level held mercantile establishments, with large panes of glass for displaying goods, and narrow, wooden doors. The second floor held apartments, with tall, narrow windows. The decorative wood trims remained though few retained the bold paint schemes of their heyday. The boardwalks had long since deteriorated and been replaced with raised sidewalks.

When the workmen and the refrigerator disappeared into the depths of the storefront, Jamaica turned back into her own business. She walked down the aisle behind the counter, ascertaining that everything was still in proper order. Only the ice cream scoop needed straightening in its circulating water bath beside the ice cream case. Satisfied, she returned to the kitchen and, once more, sat her butt down at her desk to work on her bookkeeping.

Her cellphone rang the all too familiar theme song to the Harry Potter movie series. Jamaica sighed as she pulled the phone out of her skirt pocket and toggled it on.

"Hi, Daddy," she answered, her voice lighter and brighter.

"How's my girl, today?" he asked, his voice scratchy and breathy.

Same as I was hours ago when I was there making your breakfast. Jamaica's nerves jangled that he had somehow forgotten that fact. "Good, how are you feeling?" She picked up her pencil and twiddled it between her thumb and index finger.

"Never better, Pumpkin. And how's business today?"

"Great. Kevin Dailey from next door was just here ordering his daily ice cream cone."

"Nice guy, Kevin. Is he married?"

Jamaica clicked her tongue in disapproval and huffed. She dropped the pencil on the desk top. "Yes, he's married. Lovely wife and two super kids, Sara and Zachary. He was telling me Sara lost her two front teeth this weekend."

"Oh, too bad."

Jamaica knew he wasn't commenting on the little girl's teeth.

Silence filled the wireless connection.

"Is there something you wanted?" Jamaica fingered the pile of receipts on her desk as she spoke.

"I, um, was wondering if you're still thinking you'll be able to, um, you know, pay back the loan on time."

Jamaica cringed, eyes shut tight as she said, "Yes, I will. Why do you ask?"

"Oh, I need to make plans. You know how it is for me, Pumpkin. Home healthcare aides for my diabetes are costing me an arm and a leg."

"I'm sorry Dad, do you need some money now? I can give you what I've saved up so far," she asked, trying not to choke on the round, hairy thing that had formed in her throat. She closed her eyes again, hoping he didn't ask how much it was.

"No, no. I'm doing okay. I can wait until the date we agreed on. Just wanted to make sure it was still coming."

Jamaica breathed a silent sigh of relief. "Yes, of course. I'll have your money returned by December first, as we agreed."

"Great, sweetheart."

"Hey, someone came into the shop. Let me call you back," Jamaica cringed at the little white lie.

"No need, no need, sweetheart. Have a good day and talk to you again soon." His voice rattled before he hung up.

Jamaica trudged over to the front window pane to look out at the vacant storefront. A movement to her right caught her attention. The lean, handsome man had walked by her shop on the opposite side of the street. There was something familiar about his manner, his stride, and his profile as he walked. Then, he turned toward her and she caught a glimpse of his face. *It's Ronnie Caswell. Was he coming to check out my shop?*

Jamaica watched as he looked both ways, then crossed to her side of the street and disappeared around the corner at the intersection with Church Street. *Maybe he'd looked in the window while I was in the kitchen. Why had he not come in to look around?* A part of her was miffed she didn't get a chance to show off her baby, while the rest of her was satisfied he had stayed away.

He was back in town, but he neglected to say why when she saw him at the bar. Maybe just to visit his parents. Maybe to visit his sister or brother. He certainly wasn't here to visit her. And despite the quiver that went through her body at the very sight of him, Jamaica had no qualms about that.

CHAPTER TWO

At the monthly meeting of the Downtown Merchants Association, speculation ran wild over the new occupant of the former Fulton's Confections. It ran from fast food restaurant (not likely with the zoning regulations in town, said Michael Unger), to a restaurant, to a bakery. Jamaica cringed at the thought of a bakery. It was her hope someday to start her own bakery, a real bakery, right here in Fulton River. She prayed someone didn't beat her to it.

Vera August, owner of the Knit One, Purl Two store down the block suggested, "Maybe it's an old-fashioned luncheonette. You know, the kind with swivel stools at a long Formica counter." Heads bobbed all around the circle and a few murmurs went up from those not sipping their coffee or tea.

Warren Howard, owner of Suds 'Em Up laundromat, guessed it might be a convenience store. Fewer heads bobbed in unison to this idea.

One truck had raised the hackles on the back of Jamaica's neck…an ice cream freezer delivery truck. A cold shiver sliced through her chest at the thought of ice cream competition on Main Street, just when she was close to turning a reasonable profit.

"I don't much care who or what it is, I don't like the idea of another ice cream vendor on Main Street," Jamaica sniffed, wiping cookie crumbs off her shirt front.

"Oh, gosh, Jam. I don't think anyone can compete with you. Your shop is darling. And the flavors!" Florence Quinn rolled her eyes in punctuation of her statement. A strong murmur and vigorous nods of agreement from the crowd. "The way you have your shop set up like an old-time ice cream parlor is divine!"

Jamaica smiled. It was true, she had put a ton of work and money into making Mr. Nichols's former ice cream shop into *her* ice cream shop: the quintessential early 1900s ice cream shoppe, with a double

MELT MY HEART

P, and an E at the end. Vermont Ice Cream Emporium featured thirty different varieties of ice cream, twenty types of sundaes, twenty sauces and syrups, forty kinds of additional toppings, real whipped cream, and made the thickest, richest, milkshakes anyone had ever tried to suck through a straw. The ice cream itself, with a 16.5 percent fat content, was rich and creamy, made by a small private production company on a dairy farm farther upstate in Vermont.

"I don't care what else is being sold, if ice cream is on the menu, we're going to be having some words," Jamaica solemnly stated, hands on her hips, jaw rigid.

"I want to be a fly on the wall for that conversation," Kevin said, before sipping the last of his coffee. "If there's anyone on Main Street I don't want to cross, it's you, Jam."

Chuckles and more nods of agreement circulated throughout the group. Jamaica smiled. The day of reckoning was going to be sweet. She picked up the tray of her homemade chocolate chip cookies and began passing them around again.

She was almost looking forward to it.

***

Ronnie wondered what exactly it was the Gods had against him as his luck went from bad to horrid. The woman he hoped to run into when he got back in town was soon to be his enemy and the person he most hoped to avoid he ran into the next day.

The morning started easily enough. An early meeting at the town hall had him working with the health department official over the plans for his store. Having done his homework in advance, Ronnie knew exactly how many tables and chairs he would need for the state and county to impose rules on the availability of public restrooms. Below ten tables, and less than twenty chairs, he didn't need a public restroom. That's what the regulation said. This official was trying to push him into putting in, not just a public restroom, but his *and* hers public restrooms, both handicapped accessible, despite the fact the entire building was not handicapped accessible.

Arguing about rules, regulations, and laws on the books was one of his strong points after an education in criminal justice and his experience as a cop. He had heard more arguments about the law than you could shake a Bible at. But laws were laws, rules were rules, and regulations were regulations. Suggestions, like the one being made by this official were just that, only suggestions. And there was no room in Ronnie Caswell's budget for restrooms.

The office door opened behind him as he leaned over the health official's desk.

"Well, look at you, all handsome and grown up," a syrupy sweet voice drawled from behind him. He closed his eyes and mentally cursed. He slowly turned around to find his single biggest regret in life. Brenda Tardash stood in the doorway of the health department office. And there was no other way out of the office except through the window, which Ronnie thought looked mighty good. *Too late to escape.* He squared his shoulders and forced a smile.

"Hey, hello Brenda. How are you?" he replied, hoping to be polite but not sound too encouraging.

Brenda walked over to him, a cloud of perfume reaching him before her body did. She laid her hand on his upper arm, leaned over and kissed his cheek. Straightening, she thrust back her shoulders. "I hear you're back in town to stay. New business and all."

"Yes, new business. If you'll excuse me, I'm trying to work out some details with Mr. Paine." He turned back to George Paine, frowning at him, which Brenda did not see.

"Oh, I'm sorry. I'll wait outside until you're finished." Brenda tip-toed like a toddler, backward out the doorway, leaving the door open as she went out into the corridor.

"Sorry about that interruption." Giving Mr. Paine a pained expression, he walked over to the door and shut it, but not before he got another sweet wave from dear Brenda, waiting outside in the hallway.

Forty-five minutes later, Ronnie stepped out of the office, only remembering at the last second, who might still be waiting for him. Brenda Tardash jumped up from a chair out in the corridor and rushed over to throw her arms around him.

"Ronnie Caswell, I can't believe it's really you! When I heard you were back in town, I told myself, I had to find you and say hello. It's been so long and you don't look a day older." Brenda strode alongside Ronnie as he walked down the hall to the stairs. Her little kitten heels clacked along the polished linoleum tile floor, her mini skirt impeding her stride. Her chest, stuffed into a halter top, heaved as she gasped, rushing to keep up with him.

"Well, thanks for the welcome, Brenda. It's good to be back. If you'll excuse me, I have to run over to the store and then get some construction done," he said, reaching the front door of the town hall's foyer.

"Of course. I do hope you'll give me a private tour of your store before it opens. I would love to see it." Brenda struggled to walk through the door beside him but two could not fit. Ronnie stepped aside to let Brenda go through first. As he got through, he kept walking, not stopping to talk with her.

"Sure, Brenda. Maybe when it's ready." Ronnie flung the words over his shoulder as he walked down the sidewalk to his Ford F150 pickup.

CHAPTER THREE

Monday, one week after the Main Street Merchants' Association meeting, dawned clear and bright. An overnight rain left everything damp and the Fulton River roaring. By the time Jamaica opened at eleven o'clock, the day was already steamy with a high of ninety-two degrees Fahrenheit expected in the middle of the afternoon.

Great day for the ice cream business, she thought as she hummed her way through her opening duties. Check the temperatures of the freezers, check the stock inventory, refill the cash register with opening cash. Jamaica pulled a fresh apron from the hanger in the back-room closet, gave it a flick to smooth out any unseen wrinkles and hung it beside the archway to the front room. She smiled when she saw her reflection in the mirror. She looked like a woman from the early 1900s with her hair in a neat Gibson Girl fashion, and her long, ruffle-hemmed skirt. A white blouse with mutton sleeves finished the costume.

Her happy humming continued as she walked the floor of her shop, straightening tables and chairs that were already straight. She made sure napkin dispensers were full, spoon caddies full of both long and short spoons. Seeing everything was set, she returned to the kitchen to make more fresh sundae toppings.

It was this quiet time in the kitchen, making the great things for her customers to eat, that Jamaica loved second best. When the magic transformed simple ingredients like butter, fresh cream, and sugar with some added natural flavorings into amazing ice cream toppings and sauces. It was almost, almost as good as watching the happy faces of her customers as they ate the confections she put together for them.

A scratching at the back door of the kitchen drew her attention. Sitting on the other side of the screen door was the dog.

"Well, hello again, stranger," Jamaica said, walking over to the door. He was far too thin, with ribs showing faintly beneath his fur. "Looking for breakfast?"

Jamaica opened the screen door and let the wiry haired, floppy eared mutt in to the kitchen. "Don't tell the health inspector I let you in or he'll yank my license." The dog sat just inside the screen door and watched as she retrieved a small bowl and filled it from the bag of dog kibble in the coat closet. She laid it before him along with a bowl of water. He looked up at her with grateful eyes before attacking the contents.

"Easy boy, don't make yourself sick." She stepped back as the poor creature filled his belly. He stopped by every couple of days for a bowlful of food and a nap inside her kitchen. She wondered where he stayed on the days he wasn't with her. It didn't seem like anyone else was feeding him.

In a few minutes, he was finished. After another thankful glance, he walked over to the corner of the kitchen where Jamaica had laid down a blanket for him. He circled three times before settling. Closing his eyes, he burped loudly, then nestled into the blanket. Jamaica knelt down beside him and ran her hand along the length of his back. He was thin. His fur was ragged and matted in places. She had tried to brush him, but he wouldn't sit still for it. The smell of him almost took her breath away. He desperately needed to be groomed but that would mean getting a collar and leash on him. She had tried a collar before and the very sight of the thing had sent him skulking behind the couch.

The dog looked up at her as she pet him. His big brown eyes soft and grateful, he blinked at her a few times, yawned, then fell asleep.

Jamaica shook her head, a wide grin on her face. She had come to think of him as "Burpy" because of his routine. Satisfied he was settled for now, she washed her hands and resumed her morning agenda.

The maple praline sauce and dark hot fudge sauce were running low. Jamaica pulled a saucepan down from the overhead hanging rack and put it on the gas stove on low heat. She carefully added the maple syrup, light brown sugar, salt, and heavy cream. Stirring slowly until the brown sugar dissolved, she let it boil undisturbed. The sweet smell of maple and sugar filled the kitchen making her stomach growl with hunger as the soft sound of bubbling liquid replaced the silence. As soon as her overworked candy thermometer registered the proper temperature and the solution had thickened to the correct consistency, Jamaica stirred in the butter until it completely melted and then the chopped, toasted pecans. She dipped a spoon into the pot then raised it, watching the dark amber sauce drip lazily. She blew on it for a minute before the end of the spoon disappeared into her mouth. The sweet, distinct flavor of maple came through brightly with the woodsy, nutty taste of the pecans. Satisfied it had come out correctly, she set the sauce aside to cool, and began the hot fudge sauce that made her shop famous.

Once again, she pulled a heavy saucepan from the hanging rack and laid it on moderate heat on the gas stove. To the pot, she added heavy cream and dark brown sugar and stirred until the sugar dissolved. Next, she added finely-chopped, unsweetened chocolate, butter, and light corn syrup. She stirred the heating mixture until it was smooth, letting it boil for eight minutes undisturbed before removing it from the heat. The smell of chocolate pervaded the room, making her salivary glands kick into overdrive.

Off the heat, she stirred in the vanilla and a pinch of salt. Again, she dipped a fresh spoon into the mixture, tasting the velvety chocolate mixture as it coated her tongue with its richness. Satisfied with the outcome, Jamaica set it aside to cool for a couple hours before placing it in the stainless-steel container in the front room.

Sundae topping stock restored, Jamaica grabbed the broom and headed for the front stoop and sidewalk. She swept the front step, angling the dirt first toward the sidewalk, then toward the street. As she did, she wondered if she could adapt her habanero-pineapple sauce

MELT MY HEART

recipe into a muffin. Would it taste as great? If she got a moment this evening, she promised herself she would work out a recipe draft and give it a try this week. She was often thinking of the bakery she someday hoped to open and the unique items she would make there.

She swept the stretch of sidewalk in front of her building, again angling the broom to deposit the dirt and dust into the street.

Admiring the clean, neat look of her sidewalk, she paused to check her storefront. The window glass shone in the bright morning sun. The gold lettering, a Victorian script font, outlined in black, was beautiful in her eyes. Filigree around the outside of the window accented the script, adding to the elegance and charm of the appearance. She never tired of reading the words, "Vermont Ice Cream Emporium" and below in smaller script, "Jamaica Jones, Proprietor." In columns below this was a list of some of the goodies she offered: ice cream, sundaes, milkshakes, sorbet, sherbets, frozen confections, homemade sauces, forty toppings, real whipped cream.

Jamaica smiled. When she had left town for college sixteen years ago, she never intended to return, except to visit her parents. But life had a way of making strange things happen when you least expected them. Her mother's bout with breast cancer, and her father's failing health brought Jamaica back to Fulton River the day after college graduation.

Her father's job loss and her mother's death kept her busy after college while other graduates had been securing their futures. Her menial jobs kept a roof over their heads. Everyone else seemed years ahead in the career world. She was working hard to close that gap fast.

It had taken what little she owned, plus a bucket of sweat and tears to get this, her dream since childhood, together and running. It had been serendipity that led Mr. Nichol's to put his ice cream shop up for sale so he could retire, just when unexpected money became available to Jamaica's father. With a promise to return the loan with two percent interest within five years, she had borrowed the money to buy the ice cream shop.

Spotting a smudge on the window, she rubbed it away with the hem of her apron. Cleared away, she caught sight of the picturesque ice cream parlor within. Her heart beat a little faster and her head and shoulders straightened.

There had been roadblocks and speedbumps along the entire way, from outfitting the storefront, to purchasing the kitchen supplies and the ornate, Victorian era replica tables and chairs. *It was all worth it.* She had prevailed with her determination.

A breeze kicked up, loosening a strand of hair and swirling it in her face. She brushed it aside, turning her head to the right as she did, and saw something that made her freeze in her tracks.

Four workmen got out of a truck with a boom. Jamaica watched them struggling with a huge sign, working to attach it above the empty storefront diagonally across the street. *That's been empty for well over twenty years.*

She observed the process as the sign was straightened and held up to the building while some of the workmen attached the sign with power tools. Covered with plastic, the wording was unreadable.

Transfixed, Jamaica spied for twenty minutes until the workmen had completed their task. One man ripped off the plastic before returning to the ground. The men got into their truck and drove away, breaking the spell that held Jamaica riveted to her own sidewalk.

Her neurons fired, bringing her to the realization she had yet to look at the sign. Her eyes sprang to the sign above the door and window pane. It read – "Fulton's Creamery and Confections — Satisfying Every Sweet Tooth." It was the name of the prior establishment in that very spot a few decades ago.

Jamaica's knees wobbled. She grabbed at her broom for stability with one hand and her own window pane with the other. She read and re-read, hoping she might have seen the wrong words — as if they might say something else, anything else, the next time she read them. They didn't. They said the same thing. "Fulton's Creamery and Confections." Creamery, as in ice cream.

Fire burned through Jamaica's gut and spread up her chest. How could anyone dare to open a competing ice cream shop cross the street from her baby? Why would anyone want to do this? Fulton River, Vermont was such a small town, it relied heavily on the summer, fall, and winter ski tourist trade for the bulk of its business. Even so, there was no way the town's traffic could possibly support two ice cream shops. What on earth would possess someone to open an ice cream shop in a town that already had a well-established one?

Two customers approached her shop, breaking Jamaica's reverie. She hustled to wait on them, all the while her thoughts and stomach churned about the new competition opening across the street.

Later in the day, one of her food service suppliers arrived with deliveries. Jamaica always welcomed Dennis Chamberlain, as a competent delivery driver, a friendly face, and an appreciative customer. He frequently brought his brood of four kids, ages six through fourteen, to her shop for a celebratory treat for good report cards or winning the cub scouts' pinewood derby.

"Hey Jam, what's shaking?" he called, backing into the store's front door with a hand truck piled high with boxes of paper goods and other food service supplies.

Jamaica emerged from the kitchen, having heard the doorbell tinkling as Dennis walked through. "It's getting a little shaky."

"No doubt. I made a delivery across the street. What's up with that business?" He set the hand truck upright and slid the stack of boxes off.

"You made a delivery there?" Jamaica's voice trembled.

"I made a huge delivery there. Damn near emptied my truck 'cept for your stuff."

"Who is it?" Jamaica tried to swallow the lump in her throat.

Dennis shrugged. "Some guy named Ronald."

The room wobbled and slid sideways. Jamaica grabbed onto the nearest counter.

"Whoa girl. You all right? You've gone pale as the sky in January." Dennis moved forward to put a steadying arm around her shoulders. "You need to sit down?"

"I think maybe I do." Jamaica's mind raced with the implication.

Dennis led her to the nearest table and chairs. Jamaica laid her cheek down on the marble table top, allowing the coolness to revive her.

It can't be! It can't possibly be Ronnie Caswell! I just saw him the other day. He didn't mention anything about re-opening his grandparents' store.

"You okay, Jamaica?" Dennis asked, his hand still resting on the middle of her arched back. "You're still as pale as a moon in June."

"I'll be okay in a minute," she whispered, her head still down, eyes still closed.

And she was. In a minute, she was sitting up again, less dizzy and a little steadier.

"What did you deliver?" she asked, tearing a napkin from the dispenser, and wiping her brow.

"All the usual. Cups, napkins, paper towels, bowls, boxes, all that kind of stuff," Dennis said. "Hey, you worried he's going to undercut your business?"

"Well, the thought does concern me," she admitted. Jamaica slumped in the ornate white wrought iron chair and closed her eyes.

"His place has nothing on you, let me tell you." Dennis shook his head. "He doesn't have the wonderful ambiance you do. No taste." Dennis sat down across from her. "And he doesn't make any of the stuff he sells. He's buying it all. Besides, it doesn't taste as good as yours."

"How do you know? Is he giving out free samples?" Jamaica's eyes popped open wide, her heart pounding.

MELT MY HEART

"Nah, just stands to reason, if it ain't homemade like yours, it can't be very good. Certainly, can't be fresh like your stuff."

Jamaica got to her feet and paced the length of the shop. By the time she returned, she had one more question for Dennis.

"Does this Ronald have a scar above his left eyebrow?"

"You know, I didn't notice."

She turned away then to hide her grimace. Was it Ronnie? The coincidence was too strong. Ronnie Caswell's grandparents had owned a store by the same name in that very spot long ago. Was he bringing it back to life? There was only one way to find out.

***

The next morning, she scanned the view in front of her. Tourists were already starting to arrive to play in and along the Fulton River. Its sparkling waters ran a slow, calm current along the five-mile western border of the town before turning east. From there it ran parallel to School Street through the center of town. After skirting under the bridge on Main Street, the river water fell for the next quarter mile dropping one hundred feet before ending in a calm pool and meandering on to meet the Connecticut River another mile downstream. A boardwalk and park began a half mile before the bridge in the center of town. After crossing Main Street, the boardwalk continued along the falls, giving tourists a bird's eye view of the cascading water.

Adventurous tourists rented inflated tubes at Primrose Point a couple miles upriver of the bend. They enjoyed a gentle, floating experience until they turned the bend in the river where they were scooped out long before they could hit the falls. The more sedate enjoyed strolling the boardwalk.

Jamaica marched up Main Street past the old buildings that were on the National Register of Historic Places. The buildings dated back to an earlier era romanticized by novels and movies. The street's most prominent feature was its wooden walkway, raised up off the level of the roadway. Some called it a boardwalk. Others called it a sidewalk. Whichever it was, it drew tourists and locals down Main Street past the small, independently owned shops that filled the buildings.

"Jamaica!" a female voice called out from the park area on her left. Her eyes searched, spotting Regina 'Gina' Maxwell.

Walking toward the woman seated on a bench with a travel mug in hand, she smiled. "Good morning, Gina. How's it going?"

"Not bad. Just enjoying the sunshine before I disappear into the shop for the next ten hours."

Jamaica sat down on the bench beside her friend. "I hear ya. I'm running an errand before I open for the day." Her eyes shifted up to look over Gina's shoulder, back at the storefront under renovation down the street. "Say, you wouldn't happen to know anything about that storefront across the street from you, would you?"

Gina glanced over her own shoulder. "No. Sorry. Nothing except it's been a beehive of activity lately every time I look out my window, which I'm sorry to say doesn't happen very often." Perhaps seeing the question in Jamaica's eyes, she added, "I'm usually in the back room putting arrangements together."

Rolling her eyes, Jamaica nodded. "Of course. How's business been?"

"It's the slow time of the year, but people still get sick, have birthdays, and have funerals. Everyone needs a floral arrangement sooner or later." Regina upended her mug downing the last of her beverage. "Well, I should let you get going. And I need to get my tush in gear too."

The two women hugged before heading their separate ways.

Jamaica crossed the bridge over the river, not giving it even a cursory glance. Her eyes were focused on her destination just ahead where Main Street crossed School Street and continued on as North Main Street.

MELT MY HEART

The red-brown and gray sandstone façade of the Fulton River Town Hall gave little welcome to any visitor. Built in the early 1920s, the elements of Greek revival and federal architecture had an odd harmony to them. Like step siblings, they somehow got along but not quite. Short and squat, it impressed without overwhelming.

Taking the stairs two at a time, Jamaica hoped to make it into the building as it opened. With any luck, she could have her answer and be back in her shop to open the doors on time.

Perusing the directory just inside the front door, it directed her to room 106, where the town clerk's office was located. Jamaica would start her inquiry there.

The old wood door was propped open. Before her stood a tall counter, behind which were four desks, each with a female employee. An older woman with short gray hair in the latest granny style approached the counter to meet Jamaica.

"May I help you?"

"Yes, I hope so. I wanted to inquire about the new occupant of the vacant storefront on Main Street. Where can I get information on the proprietor and the new business going in there?" Jamaica asked.

"I can tell you we have a new business registered for that space. Let me pull up the information on it or would you like a printed copy of it? It's a fee of five dollars."

"Perhaps you could tell me about it."

"Oh, of course." The woman walked to her desk and began typing on her computer keyboard. In a few seconds, she had the information.

"Okay. The new business is called "Fulton's Creamery and Confections." It's going to serve candy and ice cream."

"What about the owner's name?" Jamaica tapped her finger nails on the countertop.

"The owner's name, let me see...oh here it is. It's Ronald Caswell from Fulton River, Vermont."

Jamaica's vision spun and her throat went dry. She grasped the edge of the counter to steady herself. *Ronnie Caswell. Ronnie Caswell! How dare he? Didn't he know her shop was across the street? Or was that the point?*

"There isn't much else here on the business card other than an address for the business. Perhaps the zoning and assessor's offices have more information they can give you." The woman gave a tentative smile and came to the counter. "Is there anything else I can do for you?"

"No, thank you. You've been very helpful," Jamaica backed out the door, stumbling over the doorframe as she left.

Is there anything else I want to know? —Why not?

She walked back to the directory, and memorized the room numbers for the assessor's and the zoning offices.

The man at the zoning desk could only say that the business was properly suited for the zoning in the area. It had passed the requirements of the zoning board in a meeting eight weeks ago.

"We gave notice in the local paper," the official reported with a shrug of one shoulder.

Jamaica silently chastised herself for not paying more attention to the local news and goings-on.

The assessor's office could only tell her the equipment the business was said to own, which wasn't much more than two refrigerated display cases and two freezer cases. Beyond that, the only other materials listed were six tables, a dozen chairs, a computer, and a cash register.

Okay, there is not going to be much sit-down service. Not like her shop that had a dozen tables and eighteen chairs.

A quick glance at her watch proved it was getting close to opening time. Jamaica gathered up her notes and headed out the door. In her brief walk down Main Street to her own shop, she contemplated the situation.

Ronnie Caswell was back in her town, like it or not. His shop was going to provide direct competition to her own, at least in the ice cream department. She suddenly wished she knew exactly what flavors he was serving and where he was sourcing his ice cream. So far, no trucks had made any food product delivery that she could determine.

Maybe, just maybe, I can get Kevin Dailey to go scope it out for me. Let me know what's being served. I need to make sure what I'm serving is far better than anything he can serve.

That shouldn't be too hard, you make a lot of your own flavors and source your ice cream from a small, private, production company.

Jamaica was staring at Ronnie Caswell's store when she was nearly knocked over by a woman coming out of Carlotta's Beauty Salon.

"I'm so sorry," both women said as they straightened up, grasping each other's forearms.

"Oh, my God, just the person I was coming to see!" They instantly let go of one another.

"Oh, and why is that Brenda?" Jamaica asked, crossing her arms over her chest. *Great, just my luck to run into Brenda Tardash.* She couldn't help noticing Brenda was still wearing the same type of slutty clothes as she did in high school: skimpy halter top, too much cleavage showing, and a skirt much too short.

"Did you hear the news? Ronnie Caswell is back in town! He's opening the store across the street called Fulton's Creamery and Confections."

"Isn't that wonderful?" Jamaica sneered. *I'll bet you've already tried to sink your nails back into his flesh. And tried to get him back into your bed.*

"He looks so incredible. He's an ex-cop and he looks like a commando or navy seal or something, all muscular and fit. He gives me the shivers." Brenda shimmied to make her point.

"Good for you." Jamaica cringed inside.

"He's going to settle down in town again. Isn't it great? I talked to him in his store. It was like all those years in between didn't happen."

Beaming ear to ear, Brenda clicked her heels together. "There's no place like home, you know?"

"Yeah." *I'll bet it was just like yesterday. You two slobbering all over each other in a dark corner. Getting it on in a broom closet. Maybe they already christened the new store.* Jamaica cringed. *Eew.*

"Well, I got to get going. We're having dinner tonight. I'm so excited I can hardly breathe! I had to get my nails redone." Brenda flashed her hands and wiggled her fingers.

"Great, well, have a nice time catching up. Enjoy your dinner," Jamaica muttered and continued on down the sidewalk to her store.

She couldn't believe he'd still be interested in Brenda, but since he was back in town and didn't have a wife or girlfriend, she would be an easy lay. Just like during high school. Clearly Brenda hadn't changed much since then. Gained a few pounds maybe but hadn't everyone?

If he's interested in Brenda, he certainly hasn't changed much either, no matter how grown up he looks. And he was opening a store with products in competition with her own shop.

No, Ronnie Caswell still didn't have much good sense or taste. And he still couldn't be trusted.

CHAPTER FOUR

Jamaica stood outside her shop's front door; her right hand sunk deep into her hand bag searching for her keys. Once found, she set the key into the lock of the dead bolt. A car backfired at the intersection down the street, making her glance over her shoulder. She watched the car disappear through the intersection at Main and School Streets. Her eyes spotted Ronnie Caswell's storefront. There was no one around or inside from the looks of it. The oppressive heat was already curtailing foot traffic.

An overwhelming itch to look in the store window ran through her from head to toe. Jamaica relocked her door and walked down the sidewalk on her side of the street in the direction of Caswell's store. Ahead of her and on the other side of the street, there was no one else on the sidewalk. She stopped to look in the window at Tony's Pizzeria, directly across the street from Caswell's store. She glanced to the left down the street. A single car passed through the intersection a block away but didn't turn up Main Street. No one was in sight. She glanced to the right. Again, she found the street devoid of pedestrians and traffic.

Stepping off the curb, Jamaica crossed the street to Caswell's storefront. She stopped in front of the enormous front window pane. The window was still covered with paper from the inside, except for two small areas up high. Jamaica stood on her toes, trying to see inside. She was too short. Hands planted on her hips, she moved to the store's front door. Here, the paper had been cleared away at a level she could see through. Cupping her hands around her eyes, she peered inside.

The walls, a bright blue color, still showed signs of recent painting. Blue painter's tape covered the edges of the baseboards, doorframes, and crown mouldings. Drop cloths lined the floors along the walls, protecting the large black and white checkered tile flooring. Bits of cardboard, plastic wrap, and rags littered the dusty floor.

Along the far wall, Jamaica could see a doorway to, presumably, a back room. Also along this wall were two beautiful stainless-steel and glass refrigerated display cases. Jamaica wondered if they might hold the candy. But what kind of candy? Fancy, dipped and covered chocolates and truffles? Fudge and bark? Such fancy display cases would hardly be necessary for penny candies or normal bar candies like one would find in a convenience store. They had to be for fancy chocolates.

Jamaica had a flash of memory of the original store on this site. Ronnie's grandparents' store had sold both penny candies and high-end chocolates. And ice creams. *Is Ronnie trying to re-create his grandparents' store?*

Jamaica closed her eyes and tried to remember the old Fulton's Confections store of her youth. The first memory that struck her was the smell. There was a heavenly smell inside that store. A sweet, velvety chocolate aroma that enveloped you as soon as you walked in the door. She giggled with the realization that her own shop smelled that way. What a coincidence.

She closed her eyes. A vision of the red and white striped awnings over the front windows, providing shade and shelter from the rain during inclement weather filled her mind. The inside was always spotlessly clean, with a soda fountain and ice cream counter on the right. Bright red stools lined up before a brick red Formica countertop. The ice cream freezers and all the condiments and soda fountains lined up along the wall facing the counter. Grandpa Caswell in a white uniform ready to fill any order while Grandma Caswell sat at the cashier stand to the right inside the door.

Along the left wall were the glass and wood display cases filled with plates of fancy chocolates. Ginger jars of penny candy sat on shelving along the wall behind the cases, out of the reach of hungry children. It was a typical early 1950s soda fountain. They never renovated it, as far as Jamaica could remember. How she had loved that store as a child. It was the highlight of her week to spend her allowance money there. She'd spend a long time, walking the aisle, looking at all the candy choices and the ice cream flavors.

She vaguely remembered it shutting down when she was a little girl but didn't know why. She had always assumed Grandma and Grandpa Caswell grew too old to take care of the store and no one in the family wanted to take over. Ronnie's father was an only child and was employed with Green Mountain Power Company as a lineman at the time. Leaving such a steady job, health insurance, and a pension to take over the family business would have been foolhardy. Jamaica opened her eyes and wondered at the transformation Ronnie had made.

Along the right wall was a counter much like her own, except this was stainless steel instead of marble. A sneeze shield over the counter gave Jamaica the impression the counter would hold the ice cream tubs. Above the shield, hanging from the ceiling were modern style hanging pendant light fixtures with multi-colored shades.

Stacked in the center of the room were red folding bistro chairs and bright blue small bistro tables. The chairs lay folded and stacked while the tables sat paired, one upside down on top of its mate. The décor was nothing like his grandparents' store. The 1950s look with wainscoting, a long counter with swivel stools and a mirrored back wall were gone.

The longer Jamaica looked, the more unsettled her gut grew. The place looked too modern and almost ready to open. Steam rolled through her body up to her ears.

Unable to stand the sight any longer, Jamaica turned around.

She gasped.

Standing on the sidewalk, five feet away, was Ronnie Caswell. His light brown hair was neatly parted on the side and swept to the left, as it had been the last time Jamaica had seen him at O'Toole's Tavern. A blue polo shirt and boot cut jeans accentuated his fit build. He was muscular, taut, and lean. His blue-green eyes watched her without blinking, a hand on his hip. He looked every inch as edible today as he did back in high school. Maybe better. Jamaica let her eyes wander the length of him. Her body quivered with the memory of being held tight against that fine chest, then opening her eyes after a sultry kiss, seeing those blue-green orbs staring into hers. The memory took her breath away.

Jamaica couldn't do anything but stare, her mouth gaping open.

"Hello, Jamaica," he said wryly.

Still, Jamaica couldn't respond. She did close her mouth and swallow the lump curdled in her throat.

"Long time, no see. Do you like the store so far?"

At the reference to his store, the built-up steam came bursting out of Jamaica unabashed. "I can't believe you have the gall to show your face. No, wait, I do believe you're stupid enough to do such a thing. Why didn't you tell me you were opening an ice cream store?"

"Tsk, tsk. Me thinks the lady is angry." He crossed his arms over his chest, planting his left foot forward and shifting his weight to his right leg.

"You haven't seen angry yet, bucko. What do you mean by opening an ice cream shop across the street from mine? Are you trying to antagonize me? Put me out of business? Well, let me tell you, it won't work. I've been running the Emporium in this town for five years now and the people of this town love my shop and everything I provide. Don't even think of trying to compete with me, because, buster — you're going to lose."

Ronnie stood straighter and held his right index finger in the air. "First off, this is where my grandparents used to have their store. I'm re-opening it with a few modifications. Second, I didn't have any idea you owned the Emporium. Third, I think the people of this town have a right to see what they're missing. You're certainly not providing them with quality chocolates. You're a one trick pony in a large horse show."

Jamaica stood on her toes, getting eye to eye, six inches from Ronnie Caswell's nose. Her heart momentarily seized staring into his eyes before her anger took over again. "I'll show you a thing or two about toeing the line in a small town. In a few months, you'll be wishing you never set foot back in this town, never mind re-opened a business here. There was a reason it went out of business in the first place. Because the Emporium is better." And she stomped across the street to her own store.

She felt the pair of blue-green eyes watching her every step to her own door. She tried not to fumble with the keys, but it took several attempts to put the right key in the lock. Opening the door, she slipped inside and dropped into the nearest chair. *God help me! Those are still the most incredible eyes I've ever seen.* She dropped her head into her hands and began to sob. *It has been nearly sixteen years and he still makes me senseless.*

"What am I going to do?" she asked out loud. She looked around her shop, her baby. Everything was white and neat and so damn perfect. The décor was perfect, the menu was perfect, and the entire ambiance was perfect. Why, oh why, did he have to come back into her life, and why did he have to threaten her very existence?

A knock on the front door startled Jamaica to her feet. On the other side of the glass door was Kevin Dailey. She waved him in.

He gingerly approached Jamaica where she stood rooted to the floor "I saw you having words with the new proprietor across the street. They didn't look friendly. Is everything okay?"

Jamaica wiped her eyes with her hand. "Ah, yeah. We had words. We're well acquainted with one another from a long time ago."

Kevin's eyes widened. "Really? Did he know you were here or was it a total surprise?"

"Oh, I'm sure he knew I was here and knows exactly what he's trying to do."

"Which is?" Kevin cocked his head to one side.

Jamaica's shoulders slumped forward, and tears welled in her eyes again. "Put me out of business."

CHAPTER FIVE

The showerhead spray hit Jamaica square in the face. *Damn, should have turned it on before I got in.* She shivered. *No, I never would have gotten in the cold shower.* Trembling head to toe, she stood and took the beating of the cold water, willing the hot water to hurry its way through the pipes. Rather than prolong the agony, she soaped up and rinsed off, then wet her hair.

By the time she had shampooed, hot water was pouring from the spout. *God, I hate waking up this way.* Truth was, it was the most effective manner to awaken and shower, saving time. *Then stop hitting snooze and get up on time.* Rinsing the conditioner from her hair, she luxuriated in the steaming water for a few seconds before shutting it off.

Never one to dally over her appearance in the morning, she was in the car within fifteen minutes. She drove the few minutes to her father's apartment, all the windows in the car down, letting the soft, warm morning air soothe her nerves and dry her hair at the same time. Pulling into the senior housing complex, she parked in her father's visitor spot and hustled to the door. It opened the second she stepped on the landing.

"You're late. Again." His gruff voice welcomed her as he walked away, heading for the kitchen. "Help me."

Jamaica's heart lurched in her chest and she sprang forward to catch up with him. "What's wrong? Are you all right?"

Her father nodded in the direction of the kitchen.

Jamaica hastened in, finding the coffee maker spewing fresh hot coffee all over the countertop and floor. "Where's the coffee pot?" She asked, jumping forward, unplugging the machine from the wall socket.

"Now, if I knew that, there wouldn't be a problem, would there?" He crossed his arms over his chest, watching as she snatched up every dish towel she could find to sop up the coffee puddling on the countertop and running down the cabinets to the floor.

"Didn't we put it in the dishwasher for a cleaning last night?" Jamaica huffed over her shoulder.

Her father stepped around her, opened the dishwasher and looked up. "There it is!" He pulled it out and held it up.

Jamaica's teeth clenched tight. She couldn't yell at him. It wouldn't do any good. It was yet another example of how his mind was slipping away. The geriatrician has said these types of episodes would happen with increasing frequency. The meds her father took were meant to stave off the dementia. Some days they worked better than other days.

"I thought this coffeemaker had some sort of toggle switch to stop coffee from flowing when the pot wasn't there." Jamaica examined the coffeemaker for damage. She couldn't find any. "Dad, leave it unplugged today so it can dry out, okay?"

"What about my morning coffee?" He sat down at the tiny kitchen table.

"How about tea today?" She put a smile on her face and started microwaving a mug of water.

Sydney Jones grumbled, muttering to himself as his daughter made his tea and then doled out his morning pills.

"Still on your oatmeal kick?" She asked him, a pot in hand.

"You bet. Good for my heart and my digestion. Your mother always made me oatmeal." He sniffed, reached in his pocket for a handkerchief, blew his nose lightly and stuffed it back.

Jamaica made his oatmeal, remembering as she did, all the times she sat at their big, old Formica-topped kitchen table in the old house, and watched her mother make her oatmeal for breakfast. An ache throbbed deep in her chest remembering how her mother would always ask her what she wanted to put it her oatmeal. Every morning, it was a game they played. It started out real enough with chocolate chips being a frequent request. One morning, Jamaica got silly and asked for an elephant. Her mother complied, pretending to pull an elephant out of the refrigerator and dropping it into her oatmeal bowl. After that day, the sky was the limit for Jamaica's five-year-old mind.

"How about an egg? You could use some protein for breakfast." She tossed a few eggs into a pot of boiling water.

"No, thanks." He said, scraping the bowl with his spoon, trying to snag every bit of oats.

Jamaica smiled. He always declined the hard-boiled eggs at breakfast. Every morning she left them in a bowl on the kitchen table and the bowl was empty the next morning. Meals on Wheels delivered her father's lunch, but it didn't arrive until almost one o'clock, six hours from now. The eggs and the fruit she kept stocked in the bowl on the counter would tide him over until his meal arrived.

The eggs jiggled in the pot as they boiled. Jamaica sat across from her father at the table.

He set his empty bowl down and picked up his tea mug. "Aren't you going to have some breakfast with me?"

"Not today. I'm running late."

"I'll say." He took a sip of his tea and stared at her.

Choosing to ignore him, Jamaica shut off the burner, cooled the eggs and laid them out. Then she walked around the apartment, picking up trash, dirty dishes, and glasses. In the bedroom she made his bed and picked his dirty clothes off the floor, putting them into the hamper.

When all was neat and tidy, she glanced at her watch. "Hey, Dad. I'll empty the dishwasher tomorrow morning. Leave the dirty dishes in the sink, okay?"

Sydney shuffled back to the living room and collapsed into his recliner, remote in hand. "Yup." He switched on the television, the sound blasting throughout the tiny apartment.

She kissed his forehead. "I'll see you later."

He was already too absorbed in the morning news to pay her any more attention. Jamaica slipped out the door, her eyes watering. *Be grateful his diabetes is under control with medication, even if his dementia isn't.* She blinked rapidly to clear her vision. Some mornings, like today, were not so good. He seemed to have skated along between reality and his own world for a long time. Now, it was fifty-fifty. Jamaica shivered thinking that one of these days, he'd slip away and never return. Not even for her.

***

The nutty smell of burning butter brought Jamaica back to reality. Not that she wasn't thinking about reality. The chances of bankruptcy were very real if Ronnie opened his shop. But her immediate reality was a pot of scorched butter, sugar, and corn syrup instead of the makings of her delicious butterscotch sauce.

Wincing at her second burned pot of the morning, she scraped the mess into the trash can and brought the pot to the sink where it joined its twin for a soak in soapy water.

Jamaica stared out the window to the parking lot behind the building. Then she caught sight of her reflection in the windowpane. Her hair was frizzed out from beneath her kerchief and her eyes looked deep set and dark from lack of sleep. *Get a grip girl or you'll be putting yourself out of business making things over and over again. Forget about Caswell and his store for a few hours. And forget about those eyes.*

She turned back to the kitchen, pulled another pot from the rack and started to assemble the butterscotch sauce yet again. She measured and stirred sugar, corn syrup, butter, and a pinch of salt over medium heat. Eyes focused and mind concentrating on the sugar dissolving in the bottom of the pot, she waited until it began to boil and stopped stirring. She stuck her candy thermometer in the liquid and monitored it closely, not taking her eyes from the line of numbers on the thermometer until it registered 280 degrees Fahrenheit.

Taking the pan gingerly in both pot-holder clad hands, she moved it off the heat and stirred in the heavy cream. Adding the vanilla and finally, the splash of fresh lemon juice, the aroma of butterscotch leapt from the pot, filling the kitchen. A huge sigh escaped her lips as she put the pot aside to cool completely. *Thank you God, for helping me finish this one task this morning.*

There was still the chocolate mint sauce to make, as well as a batch of chocolate chip cookies for her chocolate chip cookie ice cream sandwiches. And a batch of brownies for the brownie sundaes. And a double batch of mango sorbet. Jamaica rolled her eyes to heaven and closed them. *If only I had the energy.* There was no excuse for not making the items needed for the shop. She had only herself to count on. No one else was going to do it. There was no one else who would help her. So far, the finances of the shop didn't allow for additional help. It was all on her shoulders and it was weighing heavier with each passing year.

The shop was bringing in enough to pay the bills. It wasn't bringing in enough to pay for any help. Nor did it allow her to save much to repay the loan her father had given her. Plopping down on the nearest chair, and slumping against the seatback, she closed her eyes and searched for strength. A little voice in her head called out, "How much longer can you carry all this?" Jamaica shook her head to rid the recesses of her brain of the blasphemous creature.

Her attention was drawn over to the corner where Burpy slept. The dark brown, wiry haired dog had shown up this morning exceptionally hungry after a four-day absence. After his first bowl of kibble, he had sat back on his haunches, his brown eyes silently begging for more. Jamaica had complied. Now, she observed the dog's chest rise and fall rhythmically in slumber and tried to calm herself. If she failed, who would feed Burpy?

"This isn't getting me any closer to done before opening time," she said out loud. She stood, kicked the chair into its corner by the desk and reached up on the shelf for her baking recipes. First, she'd start the cookies. Next, the brownies. While the brownies baked, she'd make the chocolate mint sauce. The last item on her list was mango sorbet. She'd peel and chop the crate of mangos. By then, it would be opening time. Rarely did she have customers earlier than eleven-forty-five, giving her mango mixture the time it needed in the sorbet freezer.

Jamaica went to work. It wasn't until she was done and standing beside the front door, unlocking it, that she saw the sign that would send her mind back into its morning tailspin.

It was a glance. Just a happenstance glance over toward Caswell's storefront. And there it was. A large, sandwich-board sign, nearly five-feet-tall and four-feet-wide by her estimation. It proclaimed Saturday as the "Grand Opening" of "Fulton's Creamery and Confections."

Heat surged through her body, the pressure of it threatening to explode out through the top of her head. Overcome with emotion, she forgot her ice cream, forgot opening the store, forgot everything.

Jamaica flung open the front door, strode across the street and over to the sandwich board sign. She looked up at the store window. There, perfectly framed in the front window of Ronnie's store, was Brenda Tardash leaning into Ronnie for a kiss. Jamaica turned away, her hands fisted and her teeth clenched.

She looked at the sign, first at one side, then the other, which said the same thing. Arms crossed over her chest, she glared at the sign, and up at the window. The two love birds were engrossed in conversation. Suddenly, of its own accord, her right foot came up and kicked the sign, knocking it to the ground. Spotting a small mud puddle by the curb, Jamaica walked through it then stomped on the sign, leaving size seven footprints all over it.

With one last look at the sign, she was satisfied with her work, and strode back to her own shop. She turned the sign in the window to "OPEN" and went to the kitchen with a smug smile on her face. The smile crumbled as she reached her desk chair. Collapsing into its firmness, she burst into tears.

Hot tears rolled down her cheeks unabated. She did not try to stop them. Long ago she'd learned to let those tears flow, to let the sorrow, the anger, and the stress out. She let her mind rant too: *I will not lose my shop. I will not lose my Dad's inheritance and healthcare money. And I will not lose myself and find my life ruined yet again by Ronald Caswell.*

The very thought of his name made her head spin. It had been so long ago and yet still hurt like yesterday. Her first kiss, her first love, and her first heartbreak all rolled into one person.

Her mind skittered to fourth grade when she had received her first kiss from little Ronnie Caswell, the puny wimp of a kid, on a dare from her schoolgirl friends. She'd won the Twinkies and Ronnie's attention, whether she liked it or not. And it was more like not, at least until he shot up in height and filled out a little in high school. By tenth grade, she was happy to have Ronnie Caswell's attention. All that year and the next, they were a steady item. In the spring of their senior year, after their huge argument, Ronnie betrayed her, leaving a party with the class slut, Brenda Tardash instead of with her. It was all over school before she knew about it.

A messy breakup followed with tears and angry words on both sides. He accused her of being cold. She accused him of being too interested in sex, something she wasn't dishing out. It had been a humiliating time in her life.

En route to her Trigonometry class, she saw him up ahead beside his locker, watching the traffic. His eyes brightened when he saw her. An uneasiness filled her gut and she looked away, ignoring him. Moving to the far side of the hallway, she put as much distance and moving bodies between them as possible. It didn't help.

"Jamaica." Ronnie snared her forearm through the stream of students, forcing everyone to stop or divert around them.

She turned on him, her eyes narrowed to slits but still piercing him. "Let go of me." She jerked her arm out of his grasp. "Don't touch me."

MELT MY HEART

The swarm encircled them. They whispered, giggled, laughed, heckled. The guys egged Ronnie on. The girls shook their heads with disapproving looks and sneers.

"Jamaica." Ronnie started again, stepping closer.

"Stop." She looked around, her claustrophobia activated, her heart racing, her mouth dry, and her eyes shifting rapidly around the circle surrounding them. Her breath came in pants as her eyes scoured the crowd searching for egress. The pounding in her chest accelerated. There wasn't any escape.

Ronnie grabbed her arm again, turning her back toward him.

Her fist flew out, aiming for his face.

He dodged.

Missing, she fell forward, spinning in mid-air, landing on her ass, her books scattering all over the floor. Ronnie offered her a hand, she slapped it away.

Sobbing outright, she sat on the floor, unable to move because of the crowd. The mob erupted, taunting and heckling her. Brenda got in her face. "You messing with my man?"

A team of teachers broke up the crowd. Tears still spilling down her cheeks, Jamaica was helped to her feet and escorted to the nurse's office.

It was three days before she could return to face her schoolmates. Then she had to watch Ronnie walking down the halls between classes with Brenda in hot pursuit the remainder of the school year.

Now, here she was, just as betrayed and humiliated. This time in front of an entire town full of people she hoped had come to like and respect her. And here she was doing stupid things like kicking over sandwich board signs.

Jamaica prayed no one saw her do it. Even if he had not seen her, no doubt Ronnie would know who had tampered with his sign. Heck, he might have watched her do it.

Jamaica sniffled. She grabbed a tissue from the box on her desk and blew her nose.

She wasn't the least bit sorry. Ronnie had no business starting a competing business here in her town. Whatever his motive was, it was wrong, it was evil, and it had to stop.

The tinkle of the front door bell brought Jamaica back to reality. She wiped her tear-stained cheeks, fluffed her hair, and straightened her apron. As she walked through the archway from the kitchen, she was sorry she heard the bell.

Ronnie stood in her shop, eyes roaming around the room, taking in every detail of the meticulously decorated ice cream parlor. "I thought I'd find you here."

"What do you want?" Jamaica straightened her shoulders and lifted her head to stand as tall as she possibly could. The sensation gave her courage, as she was standing up to her foe.

"Don't touch my sign again, Jamaica. Next time, I'll call the cops." He pointed his index finger her way, shaking it as though she were a bad child.

"Don't shake your finger at me unless you want it cut off. Did I break up your intimate moment?"

"Don't be ridiculous."

She mimicked, "Don't be ridiculous. Looks like you've made more reconnections since you've been back." She approached him, fists balled, arms by her side to keep from swinging at him. "Get the hell out of my shop. You're not welcome here."

"Believe me, I'm not here for pleasure. I'm warning you." His eyes flashed before he backed away. "Don't do it again."

Jamaica watched, her back stiff and her jaw muscles hard. The doorbell tinkled, signaling his departure. Once more, she went through the archway into the kitchen. Heat rose through her body as she replayed the encounter over and over in her mind. Just as suddenly, her knees began to wobble and she had to sit down in the desk chair again.

He's so…so…gorgeous. There was nothing else she could say. Sure, he'd come over to ream her out, but with his eyes flashing and his thick, sandy-blonde hair flying as he moved, he looked like a Roman god. And he'd been in her shop. She had no idea what he'd really thought of her store, but he'd gotten a look around by the time she had entered the front room. The décor was far from the style of his shop.

The front door bell tinkled again. Jamaica rose and strode through the archway to wait on her customer. This time it was Kevin Dailey, in for his own daily treat.

"Hey Kev, how are you today?" she asked as she smoothed the wrinkles in her apron.

Kevin leaned on the counter with one hand. "Good, good. Saw you had a visitor. Did he have much to say about you kicking over his sign?" He got right to the point. She could always count on Kevin to tell it like it is, without preamble.

"Yeah, said he'd call the cops if I did it again. I think once was enough. For now." Jamaica smiled a mischievous grin.

Kevin walked the length of the counter, as he did every day, reading the list of ice cream and sorbet flavors. They didn't change much though she did have some seasonal items and a special each week.

"I'll have a double scoop of the peach spice." He rubbed his hands together as he waited.

"Good choice. Coming right up." Setting to work, Jamaica grabbed the nearest ice cream scoop and reached for the tub of peach ice cream spiced with cinnamon, allspice, and a dash of cardamom.

"Well, he gave you the word. Anything else?" Kevin asked as he scrutinized Jamaica assembling his ice cream cone.

"Nah, that was all. Gave me a warning and left."

Jamaica thought a few minutes as she scooped and decided to try her luck. She handed over his ice cream but didn't take the five-dollar bill he offered. "I was wondering if you might do me a favor."

"What is it?"

Her voice dropped to a whisper, though they were the only two people in the store. "On Saturday, would you go over for the grand opening and scope out the place? Find out what kinds of ice cream and candy Ronnie is selling?"

Kevin nodded, glancing over his shoulder to ascertain no one else was there. "Sure, I'll bring the kids and let you know all about it." Kevin tried handing her the five-dollar bill again.

Jamaica held up her hand. "No, this one's on me for Saturday's spy mission."

"Thanks." He stuffed the bill into his pants pocket. "Any other stores you want spied on?" he smiled.

Jamaica busted out laughing. "No! Now get out of here before I throw you out too!"

***

The phone rang at nine o'clock. Her heart racing with the possibility it was her father having a medical problem, or worse, his medical alert system notifying her he had set off his alarm for emergency aid. She sprinted for the phone across the room. "Hello?"

"Jamaica, darling. It's Mary."

Slouching back against her desk, her hand over her heart to steady it. "Mary. How are you? Back from visiting Celeste in New York?"

"Yes, and all five of the grandchildren. I love them dearly, but two weeks was one week too long for this grandma." Mary Kettlebrook laughed.

Jamaica chuckled with her. She couldn't even imagine having one child to care for, never mind five. "Well, I missed you while you were gone so I'm glad you're back."

"I've missed our late-night discussions. And my ice cream delivery." Mary huffed. "My daughter buys that store brand ice cream rubbish. I tried to tell her to buy the better stuff, but she said it's too expensive. I say it is worth every penny. I've been yearning for yours the entire time I've been gone."

MELT MY HEART

"Thank you, Mary. I appreciate the vote of appreciation. What are you having tonight?" She picked up a note pad, pen poised.

"My favorite, please. Maple walnut ice cream with maple walnut cognac sauce, whipped cream, and two cherries."

"Oh, Mary. I haven't had one of those since you left. I just might join you tonight." She scribbled the order down.

"Wonderful. I want all the latest news from Main Street."

"We could be up for a while." Jamaica laughed again, her mind racing with the developments across the street.

CHAPTER SIX

Ronnie's cellphone vibrated in his pants pocket, giving him a jolt. All the muscles in his body tensed. Every phone call he had received this morning had been about problems.

Leaning forward in his desk chair, he extracted the phone from his back pocket and checked the screen. For once today, it identified the person calling. The hairs on the nape of his neck stood at attention. This couldn't be a social call. He never called to make chit chat. Ronnie's jaw stiffened tighter as he clicked to answer the call. "Hello, Chief."

A booming voice came through the phone. "Caswell. I've got news for you."

A shiver ran down Ronnie's spine. Chief Mercer was usually short on words to the point of being curt, but today's pronouncement was extreme. He sat up straighter. "What's happening?" He pulled the phone away from his ear to save his hearing.

"I got a call from the super at the Southern State Correctional Facility in Springfield. Standler's accidentally been released instead of another guy with the same last name. He walked last week."

At the mention of Standler's name, Ronnie's leg ached more than usual. "Any sign of him?"

"They've got an all-points bulletin out and are questioning his folks in Benson. So far there's been no sign of him. You need to guard your back, son."

Ronnie was quiet as he let the news soak through his brain. He remembered the words Gary Standler had shouted across the courtroom at his sentencing hearing, "I'll get you good, next time!" he yelled as the guards struggled to drag him out of the courtroom.

Now, the man was on the loose. Would Standler be stupid enough to come after him? Ronnie didn't know for sure but he wasn't going to take any chances.

"Thanks for the warning, Chief. I appreciate the heads up."

The voice blared, "You're a good man, Caswell. Could have gone far if it wasn't for that asshole's bullet."

Ronnie rubbed his left upper thigh. "I'm sorry about it too."

A heavy sigh came over the phone. "Welp, watch your back. And if you see Standler, give us a call. We'd love to get that son of a bitch in our custody again before we have to hand him back to the prison."

A shudder ran through Ronnie, remembering the condition of Standler after the shooting. Ronnie may have taken a bullet, but his fellow officers had given Standler a beating immediately after being apprehended.

His voice a little softer, the chief asked, "How's your leg?"

"Not too bad. I make sure I'm not on it too much each day," he lied. Since this store project started, he'd barely given it a rest other than while sleeping. There was too much to do. Ibuprofen took the pain down to a tolerable level most days. Other days, he did what he always did — bore it. Once the shop was up and running smoothly, he could give it more rest.

"Take care, son."

"Yes sir, Chief," Ronnie said, adding "Thanks again," but Chief Mercer had already hung up.

Ronnie sat for a moment thinking about Standler. He trembled as his mind relived the struggle for the gun — the struggle that ended his Barrington police career. Would Standler know where to look? It might take him some time but the man had a week's lead. Pushing his desk chair aside, Ronnie got up and locked the store's doors.

***

The eraser tip of the pencil bounced off the desk top only to be dropped back down on it again. It rebounded again and again, as Jamaica thought.

Kevin made a grab for the pencil, hitting it broadside, sending it flying across the kitchen.

"Hey," Jamaica barked, watching the pencil hit the far wall and roll under the couch.

Kevin retrieved the pencil, sat back down, and shrugged. "Sorry, you were driving me crazy."

The two of them looked at each other, grim-faced.

"Think of anything?" Kevin asked, twirling the pencil between his thumb and index finger.

Jamaica buried her head in her hands. "I can't think of anything I'm not already doing."

Kevin slumped back in his chair. "I can't either." He placed his elbow on the table, rested his chin in his hand.

Jamaica took the same stance. They stared at each other in silence.

Kevin sat up. "Maybe you need a mascot, you know, like Fudgy the Whale."

"What could I choose?" Jamaica asked. "What would be significant to the Emporium or to the town?"

Kevin shrugged again.

She closed her eyes, her brain running through the last Fudgy the Whale commercial she had seen on television. It had to have been back when she was a kid in grammar school. She had never seen a Carvel store in Vermont and wasn't even sure there were any.

"Do they still make Fudgy?"

Kevin shrugged a third time. "I don't know."

Jamaica's eyes widened and she stood so abruptly, her chair fell over backward. "That's it! My God, Kevin, you're a genius."

"What?" he sat back in his chair, eyes wide and searching her face. "What did I say?"

"Fudgy the Whale is an ice cream cake. Ice cream cakes! Don't you see — I should be selling celebratory ice cream cakes." It was exactly what she needed to boost her sales and give her the edge over her new competition.

Kevin's eyebrow's shot up as he smiled, "Great idea, Jam."

"Okay, you. Out!" Jamaica pointed toward the door. "I need to think this through — think of the flavor combinations and pricing." Jamaica ushered Kevin to his feet and out of the kitchen. She watched him as he left her shop, shaking his head with a gleeful smile on his face.

Rubbing her hands together, she turned back to the kitchen and her desk to work through the details.

The phone rang as she sat down at her desk. Snatching it up, she said, "Vermont Ice Cream Emporium."

"Hello, Jamaica. It's Mary."

"Hi Mary. Delivery tonight?" Jamaica grabbed her note pad and pen.

"Yes. Thank you. I can't tell you how much I enjoy our little ice cream sundae powwows. I hope you aren't minding making the commitment after all these years."

"No way. It's fun. I'll admit some nights I'm half asleep, but I enjoy talking with you."

"Me too. I try to keep it down to once a week, you know." Mary chuckled.

"You call me anytime you want ice cream. I'll be happy to deliver it. I can't always promise to stay and chat," Jamaica grinned. "Though I almost always do."

She took Mary's order and hung up. Delivering ice cream to Mary Kettlebrook was sometimes the better part of her day, even if it was after the Emporium closed. Mary had been getting deliveries from Mr. Nichol while he owned the shop. After Jamaica bought it, she asked her if she wouldn't mind doing the same. Over the years, the two women had become good friends despite the thirty-three-year age difference. Most days she looked forward to chatting with Mary. Tonight would be one of those nights. She couldn't wait to tell Mary the news about the ice cream cakes.

CHAPTER SEVEN

The night was hot and sultry for the Downtown Merchants Association meeting Monday evening. The air conditioner couldn't keep up with the heat generated by the two dozen bodies assembled in the VFW hall. Iced tea and lemonade had replaced the usual coffee and hot tea as the evening's beverage. A tray of chocolate chip cookies brought by Jamaica was empty within fifteen minutes of its arrival. The cookies were a special hit. The heat in the hall made the chips gooey tonight. It wasn't her specific duty to supply refreshments for the meeting but Jamaica considered it a good form of advertising and hoped it would lead to word-of-mouth recommendations for her shop.

Still clad in her work attire, Jamaica stood at the back of the room gripping her lemonade cup like it was a life preserver. Five rows of metal folding chairs were lined up before a head table for the officers. A few people were sitting, while others milled around, chatting with fellow members. She prayed Ronnie wouldn't decide to join them this evening, so she could garner some support among her fellow merchants.

A rotund man of short stature approached her with a cookie in one hand and a cup in the other. She tried not to cringe at Simon's approach. He had a habit of staring at women as if they were naked. "Jamaica, I hear you have competition opening Saturday." Simon took a bite of a cookie and chewed, awaiting her answer.

Jamaica blinked and shifted her weight back and forth between her feet. "Yes, so it seems. I'm trying to talk some sense into the man. He doesn't seem to understand he's up against my damn good ice cream," she said, trying not to grip her cup so hard it would collapse with an eruption of lemonade.

"For sure. The brand you serve is out of this world. What kind is it? From Vermont, isn't it?"

She flashed a tentative smile. "Yes, outside of Middlebury. A tiny place called Harrison's. They only supply one other ice cream shop in the whole state. It's great stuff. Made to order too."

"My favorite is the cherry bourbon. Though I didn't see it on the menu during my last visit," he said before taking a sip from his cup.

"It's one of the specialty seasonal flavors. It's only out while fresh cherries are in season. Which is right now."

"No wonder it tastes so good. I'll stop by tomorrow." Nodding, he walked off, after giving her a head-to-toe glance that chilled Jamaica.

Thanks for the warning. Giving her whole body a shake to expel his leer, she re-concentrated her efforts on the crowd. Jamaica stepped backward toward the wall. A quick scan of the faces present proved every single one of them had been in her shop. Some more than others, of course, but every one of them had been a customer at one time or another.

Kevin Dailey sidled up beside her. "How's it going?"

She tipped her head toward Kevin and whispered, "So far, so good. I was taking inventory of the number of members who have been customers in my shop. Seems like all of them." She straightened, smiled, and sipped at her lemonade.

"No doubt. I don't think there is anyone in this town who hasn't been a customer at your shop, um, well, other than that guy." He pointed a finger in the direction of the door.

She turned; her mouth already gone dry. She could feel in her bones who had just entered the room, even before she turned around.

There he was, Ronnie Caswell, standing in the doorway as though he was waiting for a herald. And he looked gorgeous in fitted dress pants and a button-down dress shirt with a tie.

The din of the room ebbed as eyes turned to stare at the newcomer.

Relief washed over Ronnie's strained face as the nearest member, Jack Callahan, strode over, right hand extended in welcome.

"Remind me to give Jack the wrong ice cream flavor next time," Jamaica muttered under her breath.

"What did you say?" asked Kevin, his gaze fixed on something across the room.

"Nothing." Jamaica drained her cup.

The hard rapping of the president's gavel on the table brought everyone to a seat. Kevin and Jamaica chose chairs in the rear of the assemblage. Jack Callahan had steered Ronnie toward the front row, possibly to be as far from Jamaica as he could get him. *Smart man, in some ways, that Jack.*

With the meeting called to order, Jamaica didn't pay much attention to the goings on. She couldn't keep her eyes off Ronnie. How he had the nerve to attend the meeting was beyond her understanding. Probably trying to drum up business, gain some sympathy with the other merchants in town. Well, it wasn't going to work. These guys would remember where their meeting cookies came from. *If they know what's good for them.*

Suddenly, Ronnie stood.

"What's going on?" Jamaica whispered to Kevin.

"The president asked Ronnie to introduce himself and tell everyone about his business." Kevin whispered back.

Jamaica tuned in to what Ronnie was saying, hoping she could keep her mouth shut and stay polite for a little while longer.

"...when I was hurt in the line of duty and disabled, I had to give up police work. My new line of work is my store, Fulton's Creamery and Confections. I sell high-end candy, chocolate, and ice cream, like my grandparents used to in that spot twenty-five years ago. The grand opening is this Saturday starting at ten o'clock. I hope you'll all stop in and say hello."

Great, let them feel sorry for the bastard as he tries to ruin my business.

Ronnie sat down as the other merchants clapped politely. They all understood the stakes. None of them had any wish to pit one store against another. It frightened them all to the core. If it could happen to one of them, it could happen to any of them.

Jamaica didn't clap.

The president, Benjamin Salters, concluded the meeting after discussion of the annual Fulton River Festival planned for next month. Everyone stood as soon as the meeting was adjourned, most filing over to the refreshment table for the impromptu after-meeting meeting. People stood in groups of threes and fours, talking in hushed tones. Jamaica could catch a few words here and there. Words like, ice cream, competition, business, disability, and her own name. Her blood pressure rising with each passing minute, Jamaica decided it was time to leave, though she didn't want to leave before Ronnie Caswell. *Best to keep an eye on the enemy, including who talks with him.*

Kevin must have sensed her growing anger, because he took her by the elbow and steered her toward the door. "'Bout time you left. You're getting beet red. Don't worry about him. No one here is going to sell you out."

Jamaica looked over her shoulder to the refreshment table. "I can't leave. I have to retrieve my cookie platter. It's empty." She feigned innocence. She walked over to the refreshment table and picked up the platter. She gave the nearest group of men one of her winning smiles and shrugged. "Guess I'll have to bring more next time."

"Great idea, Jam," they concurred.

Jamaica walked back to where Kevin stood. He linked his arm in hers and steered her forward.

He led her over to the door and shooed her outside. "Trust me, everything will be okay." He shut the door between them, then stood watching in the window. When she didn't move away fast enough, he waved her away like a fly.

Jamaica gave him the finger and smiled.

Kevin laughed and shaking his head, walked away from the door.

Outside the VFW hall, Jamaica stood a moment, taking a long look at the stars and the moon. She spotted the big dipper in Ursa Major and the little dipper in Ursa Minor with Polaris and her favorite constellation, Cassiopeia. The queen. *Give me strength,* she prayed.

She startled as something bumped against her right leg. After jumping away, she looked down to find Burpy. He was sitting at her feet, panting up at her in the darkness.

"Where did you come from, boy?" she asked, crouching to pat the dog. Burpy raised his right paw to shake her hand. "Isn't that cute? Where'd you learn that trick?" As she said it, the dog looked around her at the hall door, then skittered off.

Jamaica heard the hall door open behind her.

"Hello."

Jamaica closed her eyes. She didn't have to look to know who was speaking. The voice was the same, though a little more grown up than at seventeen, as her heart remembered him — as it had remembered him for all these years.

"What do you want?" she asked, eyes still closed. She put a palm to her forehead as though to ease a headache.

"Thanks for being pleasant tonight." Ronnie yanked at his tie, loosening it from his collar.

Eyes opening, Jamaica turned around and saw he was a yard away. "I didn't do it for you."

Hands stuffed deep in his pants pockets, Ronnie said, "Perhaps not. Thanks anyway. I appreciated not having to fight with you in front of the association."

"What's it to you? You're the newcomer. And you won't be around long." Jamaica couldn't help herself. The words flew out of her mouth.

Ronnie leaned forward. "Is that so? We'll see. Saturday will be telling. Everyone in town will have the opportunity to compare what they have been having, with what they've been missing."

"And they'll thank God I've been giving them the best this state has to offer once they try that crap you'll be serving." Jamaica stood, hands on her hips, her feet apart. A stance like a pirate captain on the bridge of his ship.

"Crap! Crap? My ice cream may not come from Vermont, but it was voted the best ice cream in New York two years running," he declared, hands fisted on his hips.

"That's only because my ice cream maker doesn't participate in those types of amateur tasting contests. I have full confidence in my ice cream, and my homemade sorbets and everything else I make and serve in my shop."

White knuckled, she gripped her platter tighter as she turned and walked toward the parking lot.

He called after her, "Go on, run away. After Saturday, there will be nowhere to run and hide, Jam."

With that, Jamaica's remaining control and patience died. She turned around and stomped to within an inch of Ronnie's nose. "Don't ever tell me I'm running away. I'm not running away, Ronnie. I'm choosing not to fight with someone who's incapable of recognizing quality." She turned to walk away.

"I know what my choices are, just as I knew back in high school. You're still sore I left you at that party."

Ronnie's hand flew up, his fist smashing against the metal platter arcing toward his head. The deflected and now dented platter clattered to the ground at his feet.

"Nice try. Better luck next time," he said with a smirk.

A cloud of foul language surrounding her as she went, Jamaica stormed to her car.

***

MELT MY HEART

She couldn't take her eyes off him. His suit jacket was off, flung over her chair. The white linen shirt was light enough to reveal his sculpted chest beneath.

"Come here." He said catching her eyes and holding them with his sexy, confident stare.

Walking toward him, she stopped inches in front of him, closed her eyes and inhaled the intoxicating scent of his cologne. His hands grasped her head, pulling her closer to him until their lips were meshed together. He slipped his tongue into her mouth, so gently, so softly. A hint of champagne lingered on it.

Unable to help herself, she sank against his sturdy chest, mashing her breasts against him. Their tongues played, sucked, delved deeper, yielding a deep moan. His hand slid down to her shoulder and continued down to her waist.

His lips fell to her collarbone, eliciting a shiver and a groan of delight. A string of kisses trailed lower to the rise of her breast while his hand rose to cup it. Drawing it nearer to his lips, one finger slipped inside the fabric of her bra, turning it aside. Her knees liquefied as his lips found the hard peak, licked it, then suckled before his tongue flicked crazy waves of desire through her. His arm supported her, her head tossed back and forth with the speed of his teasing tongue, drawing her insides taut.

Jamaica could do nothing but offer herself to his mouth. She shifted aside, her right breast aching for the same treatment. Ronnie stole the nipple into his mouth, with his eyes staring up into hers. She watched him suck it, and flick the tip of his tongue across the tawny tip. She throbbed as her insides melted, making her knees weak. His darkened blue eyes never wavered as he played and teased and tormented her.

A groan rose out of her and her hips flexed forward against his pelvis. A hardness ground against her center. Jamaica pressed again, rubbing herself against him, unable to stop.

"Come for me," he whispered in her ear. He resumed, sucking harder on her nipple as her internal pressure increased. The tension built, her breath became ragged and wild.

And she woke up.

Jamaica sat up in bed, the sheet tangled around and between her legs. Sweat wet her brow, she wiped it away with her hand.

Such a vivid dream. How could I dream of sex with Ronnie when I've never had sex with Ronnie? Maybe that's the problem, idiot.

Things would have been so different if she hadn't turned Ronnie down all those years ago. Things would have worked out so different. Ronnie never would have left her for Brenda Tardash. They would have stayed together. Maybe they would have stayed together all through college, or maybe not. It was hard to tell.

Maybe Ronnie wouldn't be interested in destroying her and her business if she had given in to him.

Jamaica lay back down on the pillows. *If he succeeds, how am I ever going to tell my father I've lost it all?* She knew him well enough to know he'd tell her it was all right, that it was okay and he still loved her. Maybe he would still love her but he'd be deeply disappointed in her for losing Grandpa Jones' bequest. He needed the money for his healthcare. She'd lose her job as well as her business so she'd end up losing her apartment too. Thank God, her car was paid for. At least she'd still have a car she could use to get to another job.

What would she do? She didn't have any particular skills beyond baking and cooking and a bachelor's from the University of Vermont in nutrition and food science. And heaven knows you needed great credentials from a fancy culinary school to help get a good chef's job or you'd be stuck as a short order diner cook with low pay and lousy hours. Or you could own your own business with low pay and lousy hours...*No. My hours may be long, and my pay may be lousy, but the shop is mine, all mine and no one can tell me what to do or how to do it. And that is worth far more than any amount of money could ever accomplish.*

MELT MY HEART

A quick glance to the clock on the nightstand told her it was three-twenty. The alarm would be going off in another two hours and ten minutes. Jamaica closed her eyes again and tried to think of nothing. Remnants of her dream kept floating back to her — Ronnie's lips, his hands, and his long lean frame. Somehow the body she remembered from high school was replaced by the body of Ronnie today. The man he was today instead of the young man he was then. The years had filled him out, brought more mass and muscle to his torso and limbs.

Jamaica remembered what he had said at the merchants' meeting about being injured in the line of duty. She wondered what type of injury he had sustained and how. There was no visible sign of injury. No scars or limps that she had noticed beyond the scar above his eyebrow from a childhood sledding accident. But it had to have been something significant if he'd retired because of it and been given a settlement. A settlement he had used to resurrect his grandparents' store.

Had he known about her business when he planned to open his own? *How could he not? They were across the street from each other.* Scoping the area for like businesses would have been part of the homework, part of a good business plan, assuming he made one. He had to have known there was already an ice cream source in town. The Emporium had been there since his grandparents' store had been there. And, if he had made a simple inquiry at the town hall, he would have been given her name.

Was this whole pretext payback of some sort for what happened in high school? Jamaica nodded her head against her pillow. It sure felt like it.

What was the solution? Neither one of them wanted to lose. Each of them had huge chunks of money invested in it.

Jamaica decided the situation had only one acceptable conclusion.
The only solution is to win.

Ronnie lay on his bed trying to fall asleep but the heat in the room and the thoughts running through his head would not allow it. He rubbed his jaw with one hand and his left thigh with the other. Between Jamaica and the hard work getting the store ready for opening day, he was exhausted and physically hurting. And his mind could not focus on anything except the fiery look from a pair of brown eyes and his predicament.

Re-opening his grandparents' store had seemed like a great idea. The thought had seemed like the answer to his prayers. Once it became clear he was permanently disabled by the gunshot wound to his thigh, he had racked his brain trying to think of something else he could do. Something to keep him happy and employed. He had always wanted to be his own boss. And ever since he was a child, he had wanted to reopen his grandparents' store. The thought became even more prominent when he had learned, as an adult, why it had been closed.

As a child, having Grandma and Grandpa Caswell move in with his family had been a treat. He believed it was because they loved him. Now he knew better. They had not only lost their business to Mr. Nichol, but they had also lost their house. They had no choice but to move in with their only son and his family. It all made sense now. Grandpa's decline into alcoholism, and Grandma's indifference as she sat crocheting away every day in front of the television set.

With this newfound understanding came a new purpose. The goal became getting revenge on Mr. Nicol. Now, the two goals became one. Opening the store would serve the purpose of restoring his grandparents' legacy and getting back at Mr. Nicol for putting them out of business and ruining their lives. As he planned it, he had every intention of putting the Emporium out of business.

Things were twisted. He didn't know Mr. Nicol had sold the business any more than he had known he'd sold it to, of all people,

Jamaica Jones. He really didn't want to put Jamaica out of business but there wasn't any way they both could survive in this small tourist town. The foot traffic was enough to keep only one ice cream store busy, not two.

On the other hand, he had everything he owned invested in re-opening the store. His entire disability, and all his savings. If the store went under, he would go with it.

Ronnie rolled over onto his stomach and buried his face in the pillow. He was going to have to make it. He was going to have to continue his plan to put the Emporium out of business even though Jamaica Jones owned it. Despite how much he wanted to be friends with her again. Despite how much he'd like to be more than friends with her again.

He was going to have to win, no matter the cost.

CHAPTER EIGHT

Florist shop owner, Regina Maxwell, stammered in surprise. "R-really? You want a bouquet to congratulate Ronnie Caswell on his grand opening?"

"Yes, I've decided to embrace the inevitable. Let the best ice cream win, so to speak," Jamaica said. She glanced over Gina's shoulder, peeping into a refrigerator cabinet at the buckets of fresh flowers waiting to be placed in one of Gina's magical arrangements.

"Wow, I'm flabbergasted!" She grasped the counter for support in feigned swooning fashion, rolling her eyes and flinging the back of her hand against her forehead in theatrical misery.

Jamaica groaned. "All right, already. Just make me up a bouquet, in a simple vase, if you don't mind. I want to hand deliver it this afternoon." She headed for the door, letting herself out before having to endure any more of Gina's bad acting.

"Wait, what kinds of flowers —" she hollered through the closed door, but Jamaica kept walking to her shop. She didn't care what types of flowers. It was a gesture. No, it would be an excuse to get in the door. If everything worked out as planned, it would be one simple maneuver in the cog to put Fulton's Creamery and Confections out of business before its grand opening.

***

At four o'clock, Jamaica turned the sign in her shop window to "CLOSED" and locked the door behind her before she exited on to Main Street. A quick walk, three doors down, brought her back to "Gina Blooms." Regina had put together an exquisite bouquet of flowers for Jamaica. It was far too pretty to waste on Ronnie but if she said anything, she'd give herself away. She praised Gina's talents, paid for the bouquet, and stepped out onto Main Street intent on her mission.

Backtracking, she passed her own shop again, walked past Kevin's Cards and Gifts and Tony's Pizzeria. A quick look both ways proved, a) there was no vehicular traffic to run her over and b) there was no one in the street to watch her. However, the incident with the sandwich board sign had proven one thing. There were people in their own shops who might catch a glimpse of her walking across the street toward Ronnie's shop with a big vase of beautiful flowers in hand. Kevin hadn't been the only person who had seen her juvenile temper tantrum with the sign. At least six people, all store owners, had commented on it to her. A flush spread up her neck to the tips of her ears and her cheeks.

Jamaica crossed the street, climbed the stairs and tried the door handle of Ronnie's store. It opened. *So much for security. At least I know I might be in luck later if I can't accomplish my mission now.*

A bell chimed as she opened the door and walked in. The odor of paint overwhelmed her senses. She rubbed her nose as she sniffled.

"I'll be there in a minute," came from the back room.

She spotted the freezer cases along the wall on the right. Walking toward them, she quickly glanced around to see if anyone was watching before she looked behind them. There, next to the junction of the two cases, was a floor outlet where the two freezer cases were plugged in for electricity. Jamaica swiftly walked behind the cases, set the vase down on top of the sneeze shield and panel, bent over and unplugged both units. She peeked up over the edge of the case to see if Ronnie had emerged from the back room yet. There being no sign of him, she stood, walked around to the front of the case, picked up the vase and started primping the flowers.

Only then did Ronnie come out from a back room, perhaps thinking a customer was entering the place. His eyes widened and his step faltered when he saw Jamaica.

Jamaica held the vase out at arm's length.

"I wanted to bring you flowers. A gesture of luck for your opening day tomorrow." She jiggled the vase.

Speechless, he took the vase from her. Ronnie finally found his voice, "Ah, it's nice. I'm really surprised." His eyes were wary. "Are you okay?"

"Never been better. Why?" Jamaica replied, walking around the store, eyeing the chocolates in their display case and the bistro chairs and tables before returning to the front door.

"I'm surprised. You know. Competition and all." He held the vase out at arm's length as though it might bite him if it got too close.

"I decided it's up to the townspeople. Let them decide who has the best ice cream."

Ronnie hitched his weight onto his right leg. "Yeah, let's let them decide. Thanks for the flowers."

"You're welcome. And may the best ice cream win." Jamaica swung the door open with so much force it crashed against the door stop. "Oops. Sorry." She shrugged and walked out the door.

Gasping in the fresh air, Jamaica tried to steady her breathing and keep from running back to her shop. She slowed her pace, *one step at a time,* she kept repeating in her mind until she was at her own shop.

Her shaking hands fumbled with the keys for several minutes, first dropping them, next getting one jammed, and then dropping the key chain again as it came free. She took a deep breath. Picking up the key chain and steadying her hands as she unlocked the door and the dead bolt. She was in. She turned the "CLOSED" sign back to "OPEN" and raced to the kitchen of the shop where she fell into her desk chair and dropped her head onto the desktop.

What a dastardly thing to do, Jamaica Jones! He's going to lose hundreds of dollars of inventory. But he deserves it for trying to put me out of business. It's him or me. I've got to win. There's no going back and there's no chance of winning for cowards.

MELT MY HEART

Nonetheless, Jamaica couldn't help crying at the deed she had done. It sat like over-spiced chili in the pit of her stomach, gnawing away at her insides and her conscience. She would have to go to confession tomorrow.

Father Michael at St. Brigid's Church would not be pleased with her and might even suggest she apologize to Ronnie for her actions. He was like that. He always tried to get his parishioners to atone for their actions with words and deeds as well as prayers of contrition to God. Jamaica wondered if it was a legitimate Catholic practice or if it was Father Michael going rogue in his efforts to minister to the souls of his flock. Whatever it was, Jamaica would not be atoning for her actions with words or deeds. And the only prayers she would be saying would be the same ones she was saying now. Let Ronnie and his shop never open or go out of business forever. She didn't care which God chose. As long as the outcome was the same.

The bell of her door tinkled. Jamaica rose, put on her white apron, and walked through the archway into the front room of the shop.

Kevin Dailey stood at the front counter. Today he didn't walk the counter as he read the ice cream menu.

"Hey Kevin, how's it going today?" Jamaica asked, seeing the dropped eyes and frowning mouth of her shop neighbor.

"Four customers all day," he said. "I just closed up for the night. Can't stand to sit there for another half hour."

"Been quiet here today too." She hated when Kevin's business was so slow. Over the years she had tried to help him with displays and merchandise selection, but he didn't have the eye for it, and she hated butting into his business.

"I'll have a Mexican chocolate today. Single scoop, though."

"Coming up!" Jamaica set to work, filling one of her homemade sugar cones with the spicy chocolate, before adhering an extra scoop on top. She held it out to Kevin over the marble counter.

His eyes widened to dinner plate size. "I only wanted a single scoop." He waved three singles in his hand.

"You looked like you could use a double. This one is on the house today. I'm feeling pretty lucky," she said with a smile.

Kevin took the cone, his other hand shoving the three singles into her hand. He licked, closed his eyes, and licked again.

"That's some spicy chocolate. I think the guy's an idiot if he thinks he can outdo you with ice cream. You have the best flavors I've ever seen anywhere."

"The Harrisons like a lot of my suggestions. And they produce the best ice cream because they produce the milk right on their own farm, organically. It's all done naturally, the way it was done back in the 1800s when Mr. Harrison's father first settled the farm. Even the ice cream recipe is over 100 years old."

"All I can say is you can — taste the quality — and I'm willing — to bet money — your ice cream is going to win this ice cream war," Kevin said between licks.

Jamaica could only smile and tingle from her toes to the roots of her hair.

CHAPTER NINE

The Fulton's Creamery and Confections' grand opening festivities were due to start with a ribbon-cutting ceremony by the mayor and Ronnie at noon. All night, Jamaica tossed and turned, thinking about Ronnie's freezers. Not that she felt uncomfortable with the action by now. Her conscience had talked itself into absolution. She wanted to see the look on his face when he realized all his ice cream was flavored cream soup. If only she could be there. With a deep sigh, she thought it was just as well she was miles away when it happened.

Jamaica bounded out of her double bed, over to her bedroom window and looked out onto the horse pasture. Her apartment was built into the loft of a garage abutting a stable and horse paddock. The smells during the summer could get a little ripe in the pasture but in general it was a pleasant and quiet place to live. Not far from the center of town, just a ten-minute drive, it gave her enough space to breathe away from her shop. Assuming she left her business work at work, which was not often.

She padded from the bedroom into the hallway, walking past the bookshelves holding the hundreds of cookbooks she collected from every place she could find them. The kitchen was brightly lit from the eastern windows. The red gingham patterned fabric hung about the windows and the small, red microwave and huge red KitchenAid mixer gave the room a welcoming, old-fashioned feel, as did the white wainscoting on the walls.

This morning, she had to clear the kitchen table of scribbled notes for the next month's menus and lists of specials. It was one of her most favorite part of her business, concocting new sundaes, new flavors, and new frozen desserts.

Jamaica closed and stacked the dozen cookbooks spread around the kitchen that had served as inspirational fodder. By the time she had gone to bed near midnight, the new menu for September was ready and the new ice cream flavors for the fall were chosen.

It had taken a while to concentrate on the task. Her mind kept reverting to the moments in Ronnie's shop, when she had pulled the plugs on his freezers. She couldn't believe how lucky she had been to have not been caught. And she couldn't believe how easy it had been to sabotage Ronnie's grand opening. Assuming he had not noticed the plugs. If he took freezer temperatures morning and evening like she did, he would have found out about the plugs in time to avert disaster. *If not,* she smiled, *I am teaching him a lesson in equipment monitoring and quality control.*

Table cleared, Jamaica left to make her father's breakfast. She wouldn't push him into a large meal today. She needed to get to her shop and get baking. If crowds of people turned up for Ronnie's disaster of a grand opening, she wanted to be ready to handle them should they decide to visit her shop to satisfy their yearning for an ice cream treat.

At a quarter to eight, leaving her father's apartment, she was on her way to her shop. Her mind already ticking away on the list of things needing to be done before she opened her doors at eleven. She hummed a little ditty as she drove the five miles to the store. Getting out of the car in the parking lot behind the building, she smoothed the bright, colorful fabric of her 1900s style dress. She felt pretty, and happy, and ready for the world to go right for her today.

Entering the shop from the back alley directly into the kitchen, Jamaica set her papers down on her desk and immediately turned on the oven. Her feet steered her toward the front room to look out the window. Nearing the window, she caught herself and redirected her mind and body to her own work. No sense making it look like she knew something was wrong. She had no idea what was or wasn't happening across the street. A smile started to creep over her lips and she couldn't contain her glee. *It was like knowing what your Christmas gift was because you had already snooped it out in your parents' closet.*

She gave herself a playful slap across the cheek and got to work. Her first task would be making more tuile cups for ice cream. The batter, made of heavy cream, butter, vanilla, ground almonds, sugar, flour, and orange zest, had been made the night before because it needed to chill and thicken overnight. She dropped teaspoons of batter in a line on the baking sheets, leaving two to three inches between them. One baking sheet went into the oven for six minutes while she set ramekins upside down on the stainless-steel table top.

She peered through the oven window. When the cookies were honey brown, she pulled the one sheet out of the oven. A toasted almond and sugar smell escaped from the oven as she hurried to insert the second baking sheet. After thirty seconds of cooling, Jamaica slipped each warm, pliable cookie over the bottom of a ramekin, letting each drape to form a cup shape. After it had a few minutes to cool, she lifted the tuile cup off the ramekin, all in time to remove the second baking sheet from the oven and begin the process again. After two dozen tuiles were finished, she gently laid the fragile cups aside to finish cooling.

That accomplished, Jamaica wandered again toward the front room of the shop. She stopped at the archway, noting the aroma of the tuile cookies had filled that area as well. She was too far from the windows to see Ronnie's shop across the street.

Frustrated with the lack of view, yet still not wanting to venture close to the windows, Jamaica went on to her next task: making profiteroles. She made the choux paste on the stove as usual with milk, butter, sugar, vanilla, and flour before adding the eggs, one at a time. She spooned the paste into a pastry bag and piped the quarter-sized puffs onto baking sheets lined with parchment paper. The baking sheets went into the oven and the timer set for twenty minutes, during which time she made chocolate chip cookie dough. The timer dinged, and she took the choux puffs out to cool to room temperature on the rack.

Two dozen chocolate chip cookies baked while she made peanut butter cookie dough. Jamaica remained busy, working to bake the cookies until the alarm on her watch sounded. It was time to get ready to unlock the doors.

She placed the baked goods in their containers, ready for use in the front room should they be needed. Noticing a smudge on her apron, she changed into a fresh, clean, white apron and went to the front door.

For the first time all day, Jamaica looked out the window to see what was transpiring across the street. It had nearly killed her to keep working when all she wanted to do was stare out the window to see what, if anything was happening at Ronnie's place.

There on the sidewalk, across the street was a small crowd of people, all looking at a sandwich board sign in front of Ronnie's shop. People stopped to look at it, then moved on down the sidewalk. Jamaica tried to read what it said but couldn't.

Damn it! She stamped her foot, *why didn't I bring binoculars to read the sign today.*

Moments later, Kevin approached her door. *Whoa, something must have happened for Kevin to be leaving his store to come see me so early.*

"Jam, you're not going to believe it! Ronnie cancelled his grand opening," Kevin said, his red hair wild about his head.

"You're kidding! Why?" she asked, trying to sound as innocent as possible.

"Don't know, only saw the sign out front has been written over with "cancelled" in red marker," he said. "Thought you'd want to know. Anyway, got to get back to my store." He stepped out the door.

"Wow! If you hear anything else, let me know," she called after him as he went.

"You bet." And he was gone.

Only then did Jamaica let her smile blossom to a full ear-to-ear grin. Pleased with the intended outcome, she skipped to the kitchen to dance a jig. But her jig was interrupted by banging on the front door of the shop. She froze, her heart instantly pounding. Could it be? Would it be?

She walked out through the archway into the front room. Ronnie Caswell stood on the other side of the front door. *Oh, no, here it comes. The accusations and threats. He has no proof. None at all that I did it. Let him speculate all he wants; he has no proof.*

He banged on the door with the side of his fist when he saw her standing in her shop. Jamaica went over and unlocked the front door to let him in.

Ronnie stood at the open door, his navy polo shirt and tan khaki pants accentuating his trim form. He looked haggard. His eyes were circled with dark shadows and his face was tense and drawn. He raised his forearm to lean against the door jamb for support. "So, you managed to ruin my opening day after all."

"What are you talking about?" She stepped aside to let him in if he desired. It might be better if he made his accusations inside her empty shop rather than out on the public sidewalk. Jamaica said a silent thank you as he stepped in and closed the door.

"Nice work, pulling the plugs on my ice cream freezers. It's perfect retaliation for trying to steal your ice cream customers away, isn't it?" He began to pace the white and black checkered floor of her shop as he spoke, his brown leather lace-ups making a soft squeaking sound as he turned at the end of his path.

"Pulling plugs? What are you talking about, Ronnie?" Jamaica crossed her arms over her chest, her eyes following him as he paced.

"Must have been yesterday when you brought over that lovely vase of flowers. I've got to hand it to you. You really had me believing for quite a while you were truly going to let the customers decide." He stopped pacing, turned abruptly, and faced her. "I should have trusted my own instincts. They knew better."

"Ronnie, I don't understand what you're talking about," she reiterated. "I meant what I said. Let the best ice cream win."

"Well, as you know, I don't have any ice cream any more. It's all in a pool. A wondrous slurry of flavors in the bottom of my warm freezer cases. Thanks to you. I had to cancel my grand opening day. Don't you dance a jig. There will be another one planned. It may take a little while to clean up the mess and get re-supplied, but I fully intend to have a grand opening celebration. Did you hear, Jamaica? Might not be today, but there *will* be a grand opening."

"That's great, Ronnie. You should have a grand opening. I'm sorry to hear it's not today." She tried with every ounce of her being not to smile.

"In the meantime, you are not welcome in or around my store. Nowhere around it." He pointed his index finger at her. "Not even outside looking in."

"If that's what you want. The same goes for you, too." Jamaica walked over to the front door and held it open.

Ronnie walked through the doorway and she slammed it behind him, belatedly hoping she didn't break the glass.

***

By the time Ronnie got to his shop, his temper had cooled down to lukewarm. He unlocked the front door and entered the shop, breaking into a dash as he heard the office phone ringing in the back room.

"Hello," he said hastily while panting and trying to control it.

"Hello, yes, I would like to speak with Mr. Ronald Caswell, please," the woman's firm voice replied.

"Speaking. How can I help you?" He sat down in his desk chair and rubbed his left thigh as it started to ache from the short sprint.

"Mr. Caswell, this is Mrs. Desman at the Fulton River Bank and Trust. We have a problem."

Leaning forward, Ronnie put his elbow on the desk and hung his head in his hand. "What seems to be the problem?" He wished he hadn't heard the phone ring, wished he hadn't been able to catch the call in time. *Next time, idiot, let it roll over to voicemail.*

"Your checking account is overdrawn again, Mr. Caswell. This is the fourth time this month."

Ronnie winced. The electronic funds transfer for the ice cream order must have gone through earlier than he expected. "I'm sorry. I didn't expect the electronic funds transfer to be presented so soon. I'm expecting a large automatic deposit tomorrow." Thank God for the monthly disability check.

"I can see you receive a regular deposit on the third of the month. This time we will allow the transfer to go through, but this is the last time. In the future, Mr. Caswell, you must have sufficient funds in your account to cover your debits," the woman implored.

A sour taste filled his mouth. He swallowed. He had a few more days to go before the new grand opening date. He hoped the opening of the store would solve his chronically overdrawn checking account. "All right, Mrs. Desman. I'll make sure there are no more overdrafts."

"Thank you." The woman hung up without another word.

Replacing the receiver in the cradle, Ronnie looked at the invoices scattered across his desk. He was a mess and he knew it. He was going to have to devise some system to manage his shop. And manage his money better. He slumped in his chair and rubbed his aching thigh. He'd never had much success balancing his own checkbook before. What made him think he could manage a store checkbook? Ronnie rubbed the nape of his neck, then started to sort the papers on his desk.

If Gram could do it, so can I.

***

She spread a thin layer of crushed Oreo cookies on the frisbee-sized disk of chocolate chip ice cream. When the top was completely covered, Jamaica placed an identical disk of ice cream on top. She gently tamped the disk down to seat it firmly. Stepping back, she made sure the top layer was level. *So far, so good.*

Next, she spread a thin layer of white icing over the top of the cake. Then she picked up the piping bag full of blue icing and began adding decorative edging to the ice cream cake. Blue icing roses were placed along the top arc of the cake. Satisfied after stepping back to examine her work, she wrote, "Happy Birthday Grandma" on the top of the cake. Jamaica critiqued her work. *Not bad.* Happy with the results, she boxed the cake and placed it in the walk-in freezer to harden.

Her new line of celebration cakes wasn't as big a hit as she had hoped. Yet every extra sale helped the bottom line. Besides, the newspaper ads had only just started to tout the new line last week. *What did I expect, a stampede?* Still, it would be nice to have a few more orders each week. The more cakes out there meant more tasters and more tasters meant more word-of-mouth advertising, her best kind of advertising.

Jamaica began making the second cake much like the first, minus the salutation. This cake would sit in her freezer for those who forgot to order in advance. They couldn't be choosy about the flavors. But it would be ready.

Should I make a third cake before I clean up? Jamaica scanned the ice cream smeared table top and the bags of blue and white icing around the table. She decided one extra was enough for today.

Jamaica cleaned up the mess as quickly as possible. Opening time was only fifteen minutes away.

Twelve hours later, Jamaica put her shoulder against the front door and leaned heavily against it while her hands fumbled with the sign, turning it to "CLOSED." She reached for the dead bolt and turned the knob to lock the door shut. That done, she leaned her entire backside against the door and heaved a huge sigh. Eleven twenty. Twelve hours and twenty minutes after opening she was finished for the night.

If only it were true! There was restocking to do, lists to be made of products to make in the morning. *The morning.* It would come far too early before she opened again.

Business had been incredibly active all day thanks to the rescheduled grand opening of Ronnie's shop. It also might have had something to do with the sign she had put out front offering ten percent off on the same day Ronnie's shop opened so the public could taste the quality difference. It had worked well at bringing in hordes of customers, many of them still holding some of Ronnie's ice cream for comparison. Most agreed her ice cream was better. One group of clever teenagers had brought in eight different varieties of Ronnie's ice cream, then ordered the same varieties from Jamaica for a matched taste test. They told Jamaica she won hands down in every category. *Yes! I knew it!*

She'd been so busy all day waiting on orders at the front counter she had not had time to look out the window to see how Ronnie fared. Looking out the window now, she saw the light still on in his shop. Likely he was doing the same thing she was — taking a breather before restocking and calling it a good night.

Speaking of good night, Jamaica went to the cash register. With a few key strokes, the machine started to spit out a long paper tape of numbers. She waited until the paper stopped coming, then tore off the streamer and looked at the bottom line. And gasped. It was more than she had made in her own grand opening. Jamaica smiled and sent Ronnie a silent but heartfelt *thank you* before rolling the tape up and depositing it on the counter. She cleared the cash drawer of money into a bank bag and dropped it into the safe in the kitchen.

She scanned the store to survey the work. She went about cleaning tables, straightening chairs, taking out the trash and sweeping the floor. By midnight she was ready to restock and inventory the food supplies.

She did what she could, finishing before one in the morning. Blurry-eyed and hardly able to stand, she gathered up her purse and went home. She fell asleep fully dressed, where she landed on the couch.

Luckily, the next morning started out with rain. Nobody came out for ice cream when it was raining unless it was for a special occasion and today wasn't anyone's special occasion. Back at the shop by nine, Jamaica set to work making more sugar cones, waffle bowls, cookies, hot fudge, and caramel sauces, before she began the task of preparing some of the toppings for refilling: Chopping nuts, crushing cookies, candies, and granola. Next, there was the task of doing the financial books from the day before, including a count of what customers ordered.

It was a time-consuming task, however, it gave Jamaica an excellent idea of what her customers were most interested in, particularly during certain times of the year. These trends had proven true over the five years she had been open, so much so, Jamaica trusted them like clockwork. It saved her money to only stock pumpkin ice cream during the fall and peppermint only during the holidays. She had all these trends and more written down in a notebook. It had become her bible over the years. She also made it a point to write down comments, criticisms, and suggestions, and act on them if appropriate.

It was after one o'clock when the front door bell rang. Jamaica entered the front room to find Kevin Dailey walking the front counter, checking out the menu and the list of seasonal specials. He looked worried, the lines of his forehead deepened, dark circles under his eyes, and a frown on his pale face.

"You okay, Kev?" Jamaica asked, stepping around the front counter to Kevin's side.

"Aw, not sleeping well. Had a busy day yesterday. Seemed you did too," he replied. "How did it go with the comparisons?"

MELT MY HEART

Jamaica busted out in an ear-to-ear smile. "Great! Everyone who tried a flavor comparable to mine preferred my ice cream."

"Yeah, I tried his chocolate peanut butter swirl and I've got to say, not only is yours more chocolatey but it has better tasting peanut butter, and more of it."

"Did he get a lot of business yesterday?"

"Every time I looked over that way, there was a line out the door. You should see the candy he has. It looks amazing. It's expensive too," he reported. "Not saying it's not worth it but fifteen to twenty dollars a pound for chocolates is pretty steep for people in this town."

"Yikes, I'll say." Jamaica eyed Kevin as he browsed the menu. There was never any rhyme or reason to his selections. Long ago she had stopped trying to guess what flavor he would order on his daily visits.

"Let me see." Wagging his index finger in the air, he added, "I think I'll try the strawberries and cream, today."

"Coming right up!" She smiled. It was one of her personal favorites and, she thought, one of the best flavors she served.

Jamaica walked behind the counter and started making Kevin's ice cream cone. "Double or single?" she asked.

"Make it a double today. I missed out on my daily scoop yesterday. Too busy to leave the store."

The ringing of the front door bell drew their attention to the entrance. In the doorway stood Ronnie.

"May I come in?" he called across the expanse of the store.

"Sure." Jamaica stopped, poised to dig her scoop into the ice cream tub.

He approached the front counter where Kevin stood waiting for his ice cream cone.

"Hang on a minute, I'll be right with you." Jamaica finished making Kevin's double strawberries and cream on a sugar cone. She handed it to him and took the five-dollar bill he offered. The register dinged as she rang it up and slipped the bill in the cash drawer.

She looked from Kevin, who had not moved except to lick at his ice cream cone, to Ronnie, who still stood exactly where he had stopped minutes before.

"Well?" Jamaica looked Ronnie up and down. A stirring in her lady parts was undeniable despite wanting to continue to hate him.

"I, uh, wanted to thank you for not making a scene or doing anything else to ruin my opening day. Though I see you took advantage of the event to drum up some business of your own," he motioned toward the sidewalk with his thumb, where her 10 percent off sign had stood.

"Yeah, well, just wanted everyone to have a chance to taste the difference. If they wanted to anyway," she said. "How'd it go?"

"Great day. Made lots of contacts. Sold lots of candy and ice cream."

Jamaica knew he wasn't going to divulge any more and he'd probably tell her that even if he had a miserable day of sales.

"Great," she replied with a pasted-on smile.

"Great." He gave a terse nod, turned and headed for the door. In a few seconds, he was gone.

Kevin, who stood watching the whole ordeal, finally spoke up. "Well, that was kind of nice of him."

"Nice? Don't bet on it. He's got something up his sleeve."

"Oh, I almost forgot! I got you this." He reached for his back pocket, then held out his hand, holding a brochure.

Jamaica took the brochure from him and looked at the front. "Fulton's Creamery and Confections" it said across the top, with a picture of the storefront in the middle of the page. She opened the brochure to find lists of the varieties of ice cream and candies that Ronnie had for sale in his new store. Jamaica read the lists under the heading for Empire Kitchens Ice Creams and Munro Chocolates. It was an impressive and thorough list for such as small store. Not that Ronnie had the breadth of selection of ice creams Jamaica did. Nor did he have sauces or toppings to go with them. He also didn't have any frozen confections like cookie sandwiches, one of her best sellers with kids.

The Munro Chocolates were a gourmet brand brought in from Lake Placid, New York. They had a terrific reputation and often won contests for their beautifully made and delicious chocolate candies.

Jamaica stuffed the brochure in her apron pocket to read in detail later. "Thanks, Kevin. I appreciate this. Always good to know what the competition is offering."

CHAPTER TEN

Business was down. The foot traffic was good in town. Tourists were out but most weren't entering her shop. And Jamaica could see why.

Across the street, another sandwich board sign had replaced the "Grand Opening" sign. The new sign read "Cool off with ice cream." Sitting in the middle of the sidewalk, it was impossible for anyone walking that side of the street to miss it.

Fortunately for Jamaica, the sign was also illegal according to zoning regulations. She picked up her cellphone and dialed the town's zoning office number. In minutes, she had registered her complaint and the zoning officer promised to take care of the problem.

Later in the day, Jamaica had another opportunity to look out the window and saw the sign had been removed. She gave a little smile. *Chalk one up for Jones.* She caught sight of Brenda Tardash leaving Ronnie's shop by the front door. As Jamaica spied, Brenda turned toward the front window pane when she got to the sidewalk and blew a kiss. *Gross. At her age?*

With the sign gone, sales in her store seemed to pick up. Lots of customers came and went. Most sat with their order and ate inside, enjoying the air conditioning. Some left to eat as they walked along Main Street; lined with its unique mom-and-pop shops. Downtown Fulton River was unlike any other town in the state of Vermont, with the possible exception of Brattleboro. Chain stores were relegated to the strip malls on the outskirts of town so the townspeople and local merchants could enjoy their own creation downtown.

Jamaica picked a usually quiet period in the afternoon, before dinner time, to make a few new ice cream sauces with raspberries — the fruit of the moment.

The first was a fruit salsa mix of raspberries, mango, strawberries, and fresh pineapple, with sugar, crystallized ginger, balsamic vinegar, and vanilla. Served fresh over ice cream, she experimented with ways to mix together the ingredients in a way that tasted best. It took some time, but she managed to come up with a workable solution for the problem.

Next, she made a raspberry and toasted almond sauce with orange zest, sugar, and a hint of ginger. She cooked the mixture over slow heat on the stove until it began to thicken, removed it from the burner to cool. A quick taste proved her instincts were good. It tasted great. She packaged it and put it away in the walk-in refrigerator. Only when she came out of the refrigerator did she realize how much her kitchen smelled like a raspberry patch. She smiled as she walked over to the work table and popped the few fresh raspberries left in her mouth. Their sweet and tart juiciness filled her mouth and senses.

Lastly, she whipped heavy cream to soft peaks, beating in confectioners' sugar along with a tablespoon of rum and a teaspoon of vanilla. To this mixture, she folded in pre-made almond praline. Letting it sit, in another bowl she whipped egg whites into stiff peaks, then folded the egg whites and praline/cream mixtures together. She spooned the sweet confection into lined ramekins, sprinkled the tops of each with more almond praline, and popped them into the freezer. By tomorrow morning, these biscuits tortoni would be ready to serve.

The shop doorbell rang as she placed the dirty bowls into the sink for washing.

Somehow, she'd have to get those cleaned up before leaving this evening, she told herself. She rounded the corner through the archway. Straight into the muzzle of a gun.

"Open the drawer, or you'll be sorry," a man with a ski mask ordered, flicking the steel snub nose revolver toward the cash register.

Jamaica couldn't breathe. Her hands flew in the air, in surrender. She walked over to the register under the glaring eyes of the robber and the end of the gun, opened the drawer and stepped back. Bile rose in her throat as sweat glands all over her body jumped into hyperdrive.

"Put the money in a bag," he ordered. He wore a black tee shirt under an open, red and black plaid, long sleeve button-down shirt. His jeans were greasy, dirty, and had a sickening smell of oil and gasoline.

A huge lump in her throat made it impossible to say anything. Jamaica nodded and did as the man requested, putting all the bills into the bag with trembling hands. As she reached for the coins, the man grabbed the bag out of her hand. "Payback is a bitch," he said and sprinted out through the kitchen. Seconds later, the back door slammed shut.

Jamaica collapsed against the ice cream freezers, one hand over her heart, the other over her mouth.

Just then, the front door tinkled again. It was Ronnie.

He took one look at Jamaica and ran over. He put a hand on her shoulder and searched her eyes; "My God, are you okay? What's happened? Do you feel all right? You're pale as a sheet."

Jamaica opened her mouth. At first nothing came out. She swallowed hard. Finally, on the second try, she could talk. "I've been robbed!"

"What? When? Just now?" Ronnie looked all around the store, taking in the open register, devoid of paper money.

Jamaica nodded, both hands now on either of her cheeks. "He had a gun."

"Did you call the police?"

"No, it happened, like, seconds before you walked in."

"Where did he go?"

"Out the back door."

Ronnie pulled out his cellphone and dialed 911. As he reported the crime, he walked over to the back door, but didn't touch the handle. After he hung up, he returned to Jamaica's side. "Hang on, Jam. Everything's going to be okay." Noticing how pale she still was, he took her by the elbow and led her to a chair.

She sat down and buried her face in her hands. "I don't feel so good."

"Head between your knees, Jam." Ronnie gently pushed her head down toward her knees.

A small crowd had gathered in front of her store at the sight of two police cruisers with lights flashing. It was three hours before the police left. All the while, Ronnie had only left her side long enough to close his own store. He hurried back and sat beside Jamaica the entire time the police questioned her.

The handle of the back door was dusted for prints and Jamaica had given the police a description of the robber and of the gun. They had also asked for an estimate of the amount of money the man had taken. Since it had been a rather busy day, the register tally reported she had probably lost close to five hundred and sixty dollars.

By ten o'clock that evening, Jamaica was worn out and worn down. The police had questioned the neighboring store owners. Nobody had seen anything out of the ordinary. Nobody had seen a masked robber. Once free to close the shop, Jamaica cried the entire drive home and fell into bed, soaking the pillow. The vision of the gun muzzle pointed at her head still causing her to break out into a sweat and shudder.

"Payback is a bitch." The phrase echoed through the crevasses of her brain. The robbery was payback. Payback for what? And from whom? There was only one logical answer. Ronnie Caswell

CHAPTER ELEVEN

A week later, Jamaica awoke with the ringing of her alarm clock at five-thirty. She was quick to shower, dress, and grab a slice of toast to gnaw on as she drove to her father's apartment.

She was getting more comfortable in her shop again. Initially, after the robbery, she had been jittery, jumping at the slightest noise. The bell set her nerves rattling. A single person entering the shop, especially a man, made her so nauseous she feared throwing up. The only time she had felt comfortable was when Kevin showed up, or when a group of customers came in. Now, her fears had subsided. It helped that the police had predicted the robber would not likely come back. Ever the businesswoman, she was back to concentrating her attention on her store.

To attract more customers, Jamaica was experimenting with new flavors, new sauces, and new sundae combinations. She had also delved into the creation of ice cream cakes and specialty pies for sale by the slice or whole. It meant her advertising budget doubled as a result, but it was the fastest way to get the word out about her new products. And the increased expenses of food supplies and advertising hit her budget hard with income already depressed. If money was tight before, it was in a stranglehold now. The rent was due at the end of the month, the electric and gas bills were due next week and there were the weekly supplies to pay for on delivery.

Her first task, this bright, sunny morning was to check on the solidification of the twelve pies and six ice cream cakes she had made last night. The mud pies looked heavenly with their coffee ice cream mixed in with an almond and rum enhanced fudge sauce in a chocolate crumb crust. The black-bottom pies also looked well with their chocolate crumb crust and rich, fudgy ice cream and piped whipped cream. The spumoni cakes and strawberry ice cream cakes had set evenly. Jamaica took one of each type of dessert and transferred it to the glassed display freezer case in the front room.

Next, she made the frozen lemon soufflé with fresh lemon juice, sugar, whipped egg whites, gelatin, and whipping cream. The smell of the freshly squeezed lemons gave a clean, citrus bite to the air. Once all the ingredients were folded together properly, she filled the cups to the rim with the mixture and put them in the kitchen's freezer to solidify.

A quick inspection of the cookie jar showed the police officers had not helped themselves to too many cookies in return for all their help despite Jamaica's offering. *Note to self: make and deliver a couple dozen cookies to the police department.*

By eleven o'clock, Jamaica had made cookies for the police force that was diligently working on her case, made more mango sorbet, and some marshmallow sauce. *Time to unlock the front door*, she thought as her watch timer went off. After unlocking the door, she went back to package up the cooled cookies for the police officers.

The doorbell tinkled, summoning Jamaica to the front room from the kitchen. Walking up to the archway, she paused, as was her new habit. The silhouette of a man stood in the doorway. Jamaica felt her heart stop as her breath choked in her throat. Her hand rose to cover her mouth, stifling a gasp.

"Jamaica? Are you okay?" Ronnie called out as he stood at the door.

Her hand fell as she slumped against the archway frame. "Yes. Gosh, Ronnie, I thought you were the robber back again."

"No. It's just me. I wanted to see how you were doing." Rocking on his heels, he pressed his hands into his starched, khaki pants pockets, his white Oxford shirt also ironed crisp. He looked down at the floor, the toe of his shoe rubbing at something on the floor. "I didn't mean to scare you."

Jamaica smiled tentatively. "It's okay. I'm doing fine. No news from the police, not that I expected any this soon."

"Glad you're okay, Jam. Despite our business competition, I'm really glad you're okay." He gave her a bright smile. It disappeared quickly as he glanced over his shoulder out the door.

"Thanks, Ronnie. I appreciate it," she said, all the while thinking *Payback is a bitch.*

A few seconds of silence settled between them as they stared at each other.

"Smells great in here. Like chocolate chip cookies." He cleared his throat. "Well, I should get back to my store. You have a good day." He turned on his heel and was gone in a flash.

Jamaica shook her head. Were the robber and Ronnie about the same size and shape? Clearly something had sparked her fear. Was it just a coincidence or was there some similarity between the two men? Disturbed by her thoughts, she returned to the kitchen to finish the task she was in the middle of performing when Ronnie arrived.

The day passed quickly as she cooked. By one o'clock in the afternoon, she still had not received any customers. *Highly unusual even for a Monday, but considering the slowdown in business, perhaps it isn't much of a surprise.*

After finishing another six ice cream pies: three peach melba and three blueberry cheesecake flavored, Jamaica realized the time. It was three o'clock. Not a single customer had entered her shop. She walked into the front room and looked around. The place was deserted. *Of course, it is, silly, you would have heard the doorbell tinkle if anyone had come in.* She looked at the door to make sure the bell was still attached. Yes, it was. And the door was unlocked. She opened the door to test the bell. The bell tinkled as usual.

Jamaica walked under the archway into the kitchen and sat at her desk. Quickly, she became engrossed in plans for flavors, sauces, and desserts for the winter months. And she started planning specials for the holidays: frozen yule logs, gingersnap ice cream pies, peppermint ice cream cakes, clementine sorbet, peach-champagne sorbet. In time,

MELT MY HEART

Jamaica noticed she was squinting. It was darker in the kitchen and she had to turn on the desk lamp. She checked the time; six-twenty. In another hour, she'd be closing her doors, *without having a single customer all day.*

Not a single customer all day. That had never happened in the last four years. Heck, she'd only had a few of those at all, even during her first-year open. But they had been in the dead of winter, not the middle of August. And Kevin Dailey hadn't even stopped in. Perhaps he was sick and his store was closed.

Jamaica walked over to the front door, opened it and stepped out onto the sidewalk to have a look at Kevin's shop next door. The sign in his door said it was open.

Curious, Jamaica left her own shop and walked into Kevin's Cards and Gifts. The front door bell jingled as the door opened. Jamaica could see Kevin behind the sales counter, cashing out his register.

"Hey, Kevin. You're still open? Busy day today?"

"Hey, Jam! Where you been all day? I missed my ice cream today."

"I've been in my shop all day. Why didn't you come over?" she asked, stopping at the counter and watching him count quarters, then write down the number on a piece of paper.

"I tried but your shop sign said you were closed." He stared at her as if she had asked the color of grass.

"Closed?" Jamaica repeated. She turned around and headed out of Kevin's store to look at the sign hanging on her shop door.

Sure enough, the sign read "CLOSED." Jamaica fumed as she stared at the sign. *I forgot to turn the sign around this morning.* Heat rose from her gut, up her chest and her neck to her face and out her ears. It wasn't enough that she had been robbed at gun point. This had cost her another entire day's income. *Am I sabotaging myself with my scattered thoughts?*

A glint of light off Ronnie's shop door caught her eye as a customer opened it. *I had a visitor today. Only one.* Folding her arms across her abdomen to contain the sinking feeling in her stomach, she retreated from the door. Tears filling her eyes, she thought, *Did Ronnie sabotage me?*

CHAPTER TWELVE

Ronnie stopped in front of the candy display case and looked in. He'd have to rearrange this product to make it look more even, so the diminished stock of the more popular items didn't seem pronounced. Shaking his head, he walked into the back room and sat at his desk. For the hundredth time, he stared at his checkbook balance. There wasn't enough there to order more candy stock.

The doorbell jingled in the front room. Ronnie started to get up but stopped in midair and sat back down as soon as he heard her heels.

"Hello? Ronnie? Are you there?" Brenda called out into the silence of his shop.

Ronnie dropped his head into his hands. *If I don't answer, would she go away?* He knew better. As she had done many times before, Brenda poked her head around the curtain to look into the back room for him.

"There you are. Didn't you hear me come in?" She posed herself against the curtain, showing off her legs beneath her mini skirt.

"Ah, yes, I did. I just finished counting something." He quickly put down the checkbook and got up.

"It's so good to see you again," Brenda cooed. She leaned forward, tilting her head to offer her cheek for a kiss.

Ronnie ignored the offer. "You saw me yesterday." He walked through the doorway into the front room and behind the candy display cases.

Brenda batted a hand as though striking the comment away like a fruit fly. "Yes, I know, but that was yesterday. How's everything going *today*?" She followed him like his shadow.

"Good. What can I do for you?" Ronnie began counting the different types of chocolates. He was stalling, he knew it. But to sit down might give her the invitation to stay and it was the opposite of what he wanted.

Brenda beamed at him from the front side of the display cases. "Oh, nothing. I was in the area and wanted to say hello."

How did she get her teeth so white? Clearly, she didn't drink coffee or tea. No tannin stains on those pearly whites. "It's very kind of you to stop in but I'm right in the middle of planning a supply order." Walking to her side, he put an arm around her shoulder, and led her to the front door. The doorbell jingled again as he opened it for her.

"But Ronnie, I wanted to talk to you about—" she started to push her way back into the store.

Ronnie took hold of her by both shoulders, turned her around and gave a little push on her lower back. She stepped through the threshold onto the sidewalk.

"Can't talk now. Thanks for stopping by. Have a nice day." *I thought taking her out to dinner would settle it. Answer her questions and get it over with. Even made it clear I'm here for business.* He gave a half-wave at Brenda when she stood and waved at him through the closed door. Then he watched her disappear down the sidewalk. *Dear God, if I had known returning would mean having to put up with Brenda again, I might have thought twice.*

With a huge sigh, Ronnie returned to his desk and started to resume what he was doing before he was interrupted...candy order. He calculated the revenue he would be missing as his candy stock continued to dwindle over the next six days while he waited for his next disability check.

A knock on the back door interrupted his thought process again. "Yes," he called through the door.

"Dynamo Supplies delivery," a male voice called through the heavy steel door.

Ronnie opened the door to let the man inside. He stood beside the doorframe with a hand truck of cardboard boxes which he had somehow lugged up the back stairs of the building.

MELT MY HEART

The man, "Dennis" according to the embroidered name on his dark green uniform shirt, wheeled the hand truck into the room, set it down, and slid off the stack of boxes. Next, he pulled a clipboard out from under his arm, and thrust it at Ronnie. "Sign anywhere on the form, please."

Ronnie took the clipboard and looked at the list of products being delivered. *Case of cake cones, package of chocolate sprinkles, package of rainbow sprinkles, case of napkins....*

"This isn't my order," he told Dennis.

"Let me see," Dennis said, taking the clipboard from Ronnie and staring at it. He gave the boxes a look over. "Nope, that invoice is for the Emporium, sorry. These boxes are right, the purchase order is not. Yours is the second one down. Hey, you got a bathroom I could use?"

"Sure, just through that door over there." Ronnie pointed to a door on the left. Taking the clipboard, he watched Dennis disappear into the bathroom and shut the door.

Ronnie looked at the top purchase order. *To: Jamaica Jones. Vermont Ice Cream Emporium.* He eyed the bathroom door, his heart fluttering faster. Swiftly, he took Jamaica's purchase order off the clipboard and stuffed it into his pocket. He signed his own order as Dennis opened the door of the bathroom.

"Here you go." Ronnie handed over the clipboard.

To his relief, Dennis took the clipboard and tucked it under his arm without a glance, grabbed his hand truck and started wheeling it out.

"You have a good day." He walked Dennis to the back door and gave him a wave goodbye.

"Yeah, thanks. And thanks for letting me use your bathroom." Dennis dragged the hand truck behind him down the stairs. It clunked from step to step as it hit.

"No problem." Ronnie smiled and shut the door. He fisted his hands, resisting the urge to open the door again and watch the truck leave. He didn't want to have the door open should the man realize Jamaica's order form was missing.

Back in the security of the store, he pulled out the purchase order for Jamaica's shop. The list included eleven items. Most of the products were toppings or paper goods. If Jamaica was as good a manager as he thought she might be, she would be ordering these items long before she really needed them. His little interference in her order delivery would be a slight inconvenience. More of an inconvenience for the supply company than for Jamaica.

Would Dennis remember about Jamaica's order? Or would he totally forget about it without the purchase order slip?

Ronnie went to the front window of the store and watched to see if the supply truck pulled up in front of Jamaica's shop. No truck was in sight, but then again, perhaps the delivery was made to the back door, like his own.

A lump developed in his throat as he stared at the front of Jamaica's store. He pulled at the collar of his shirt. She really didn't deserve this after having been robbed. That the incident still affected her was clear after his visit the other day. He had frightened her just by his presence in her doorway. Looking down at the order slip in his hand, he rubbed the back of his head with his other hand. His face flushed. He felt small. Caught between right and revenge. *It's too late now. Too late to fix the mistake I made.*

He stepped away from the window and walked across the store into the back room. Opening his desk's center drawer, he pulled out a packet of matches. He stepped outside the back door onto the stoop and lit Jamaica's purchase order on fire. It singed before bursting into full flame. Ronnie let it drop to the concrete before it burned his fingers. When only ashes were left, he stepped on them, shuffling them around to dissipate the little evidence remaining.

MELT MY HEART

Stepping back into the shop, Ronnie heard someone in the front room of the store. The person must have come in while he was outside. He hadn't heard the doorbell.

"Hello?" he said as he walked into the front room.

"Hello," replied a policeman.

"What can I do for you, officer?" Ronnie asked. He could tell the man was with the Fulton River police force by the badges on his uniform.

"I'm here to ask a few questions about the robbery a few weeks ago at the Vermont Ice Cream Emporium."

"I'm not sure how much I can tell you, but I'll try." Ronnie motioned the officer over to one of the small tables. They both sat down. The officer pulled a small notepad from his left breast pocket.

"You were the person who called in the incident, correct?" The officer pulled a pen from his pocket as well and had it poised to take notes.

"Yes, I had just come into the store, saw Ms. Jones was in distress and, when I had ascertained why, I called 911."

"You never got a look at the perpetrator?"

"No. He had, apparently, left through the back door by the time I walked in the front door."

The officer scribbled a note on the pad. He sat back. "That's too bad. We can't get Ms. Jones to go through the mug shots at the station to help identify him." He scratched his chin. "You were a cop, so I hear. Any chance you can help us?"

"Let me see if I can talk some sense into her, or have someone with the Downtown Merchants Association talk to her." Ronnie started tapping the table top with his fingers.

"Did Ms. Jones tell you anything about the robbery, itself." Again, the pen was poised, ready for an answer.

"Only that she came out of the kitchen through the archway and had a gun pointed at her head. The perp told her to open the register and put the money in a bag. She put the bills in the bag. He snatched it and ran out the back door."

The officer scribbled a long sentence, then stopped. "Did the robber say anything else?"

"Not that she told me." Ronnie started tapping the table top again. The steel gave a tick, tick sound against his finger nails.

"Well, thanks for answering my questions. We might be in contact again. And see if you can get someone to talk Ms. Jones into looking at those mug shots. I know the perp had on a mask, but she might be able to identify him by his eyes." The officer stood and slid the pad and pen into his breast pocket.

"Will do. Thanks for stopping," Ronnie said as they stood and walked to the front door. He shook the officer's hand and watched him get into the cruiser parked at the curb. His attention shifted to the Emporium. Closing his eyes, his chin dropped to his chest before he turned away. *It's bad enough she's not helping the police get this guy, now I'm making her life more difficult.*

Once more, he returned to his desk to wallow in his guilt and remorse.

CHAPTER THIRTEEN

Jamaica put on her apron, ready to begin working on the supplies needed for the Fulton River Festival coming up on the last day in August. On today's worklist was bittersweet chocolate sauce, peanut butter sauce, and the habanero-pineapple ice cream sauce that had become a customer favorite over the last few weeks.

For the festival, she was going to be serving bittersweet fudge and salted almond sundaes, and habanero-pineapple and pistachio sundaes. Last year's favorite sundae, candied bacon, maple syrup, and cinnamon ice cream sundaes, would also be served. Prepared ice cream cookie sandwiches and biscuits tortoni would be for sale for those wanting smaller treats.

A knock on the front door stopped Jamaica before she could begin. She folded her arms across her chest, surprised to find the face of Ronnie Caswell on the other side.

"Good morning." He called through the closed door. "I was wondering if we could have a friendly chat."

Jamaica thought for a few seconds of the work needing to be done, and then decided it must be important if Ronnie was coming for a "friendly chat." She unlocked the door and let him in.

They sat at the nearest table: an elaborate, small table much like Ronnie's own bistro tables and chairs, only in a Victorian style. Jamaica's finger scrolled along the visible gray vein in the marble top as Ronnie began to speak.

"It always smells so delicious in here." His nose lifted, his nostrils flaring as he seemed to sniff to catch every scent.

Her finger started to tap on the marble tabletop. "Thanks. Get on with it."

Frowning, he cleared his throat. "I had a visit from the police yesterday about your robbery. They asked a few questions, but I wasn't able to answer much. I wasn't here when it happened, as you know."

"It happened so fast. It was horrible." Jamaica's hands clenched on the table's edge.

He leaned forward. "I know. I was a cop, remember."

"How could you know? Were you ever on the wrong end of a gun?" Her eyes hardened and flared.

"Yes. I even took a bullet." A pained expression covered his face after his outburst. Both palms scrubbed his jaw. "Look, I'm sorry. I know it was terrifying. You had every right to be afraid. I'm so sorry you were robbed." He reached out and patted her hand. "You handled it very well. Exactly like you should. But it's over now and not likely to happen again." Sensing a plethora of conflicting emotions building inside him at the touch of her skin, he withdrew his hand.

She stared at him, her features softened, her heart suddenly aching remembering he'd said he'd been hurt in the line of duty. Cursing herself under her breath, she realized somehow she'd never thought that meant he'd been shot. That he'd faced a muzzle and not fared well. "I'm sorry you were hurt."

Ronnie looked down at the tabletop before meeting her eyes. "Doesn't matter now. Anyway, I came here because the police officer said you haven't gone down to the station to look at mug shots."

Jamaica sat back. "I don't have time, and they have a couple fingerprints. That should help." *Man, he really wants me to believe it was someone else.*

"The fingerprints will take time at the Vermont Forensics Laboratory. There's a backlog of work there. Getting a possible identification through mug shots would be a huge help. Can you give them a half an hour one morning this week? This guy may be planning to rob another shop owner. What if that gun goes off next time? Give the cops some help so they can nab this guy sooner rather than later. Before someone gets hurt."

Jamaica closed her eyes and pondered. She opened her eyes. "Okay, I'll try to give them a half hour. But I'm not telling you which day."

Ronnie laughed, "It's okay. Thanks for doing it." He stood and stretched, absently rubbing at his thigh. "I better get going. Almost time to open."

Jumping up, Jamaica looked at her watch. "Oh, crap. I have so much to do. Get the hell out of here." She rushed Ronnie to the door, locking it behind him and headed back into the kitchen.

She never saw him wave goodbye.

***

Ronnie arrived at his store to find Brenda waiting for him. When he unlocked his shop door, Brenda shoved her way inside before him. Ronnie followed but stepped no farther away from the door.

"Brenda, I don't have time right now. I have paperwork to do, supplies to order. And quite frankly, Brenda. I'm not interested in dating you."

"But Ronnie, we used to have such a good time together. We had dinner. We can have more good times together." Brenda put her hands on his forearm.

"Thanks for the offer but not interested, Brenda. We're friends. That's all." Ronnie shook off her hands, opened the door, and gestured for Brenda to leave.

Brenda stared at him, her eyes hardening. "Now I see the reason you were voted 'Least Likely to Succeed' in high school." She walked out the doorway. *Ouch.* He'd forgotten about that. Ronnie shut the door, leaned against it and closed his eyes. *But thank God, she finally gets the message. I never should have tried to be nice. She turns every nicety into hope for a relationship. Since high school, she's been trying to make our friendship into something it will never be. No more mister nice guy.* He opened his eyes with the firm belief he could stick to this approach.

?

Her most important supply order didn't come. *Not today, please.* At first, Jamaica was actually surprised. Then she was livid. There could only be one reason. *How did he manage to cancel my order? I've been so careful to lock my doors and keep him out of the kitchen when he stops in to visit.*

Jamaica paced the kitchen. Could she get by for another week without her order? Chances were the answer was yes. But it didn't sit well with her to risk running out of something. Her only other option was to call in an emergency order and pay a surcharge of fifty dollars. A surcharge she couldn't afford. Business was down, thanks to Ronnie's store. Why some people would rather have only ice cream, when they had many other options available at her shop was beyond her comprehension. Just the number of ice cream flavors alone were greater at her Ice Cream Emporium.

Something was going to have to give, though she didn't know what yet. The rent and utilities were fixed, no changing them. Her salary was actually below minimum wage at this point. It was enough to cover her own apartment's rent and utilities which were minimal considering she was at the shop constantly. Even her personal food was minimized, as she would make a pot of soup at the beginning of the week and eat it until it was gone. Not terribly exciting but far better and cheaper than canned soups or junk food.

The only thing left to cut was the menu. She'd have to take a closer look at the menu to determine what items weren't selling as well as they should and cut them out. Jamaica frowned and plopped down in her desk chair. She really didn't want to deal with it right now.

She looked at the calendar. The Fulton River Festival was two weeks away. If she had a good income at the festival, she could manage. If not, she would be in serious trouble of not having all the money to pay back her father, and she'd rather skip her own rent and get evicted.

Suddenly, the walls of the room were closing in on her. She needed to get out of there. For the first time in the five years since she'd taken over the business, Jamaica Jones couldn't stand to be in the shop for another moment.

MELT MY HEART

She picked up her handbag and headed out the door.

Sitting in her car, she couldn't decide where to go. Back to the apartment? No, there was so much to do there, it was depressing. *Just as bad as the shop.* Then she remembered promising she'd check out the mug shots.

This gave her something to think about. If Ronnie were really behind the robbery, would he be asking her to try to identify the robber? If anything, he'd want her to stay away from the mug shots. Right? But he'd encouraged her to help the police identify the robber before he robs again in the only way available.

Which meant one of two things; a) he had nothing to do with the robbery at all, or b) he knew the guy wasn't going to show up in the fingerprint matching or the mug shots.

Jamaica turned the key in the car's ignition and went to the police station.

The next day, a news story in the local paper reported progress was being made in the Ice Cream Emporium robbery case. New clues as to the identity of the robber had come to light.

***

Walking up to the white cape cod house with black shutters, Jamaica paused at the back door. *I'm not going to stay and chat tonight. I'd rather go home and wallow in my sorrow.* She looked up at the stars, her eyes searching for Cassiopeia. But she couldn't find it. Clouds were dotting the night sky, obscuring most of the constellations. She sighed as she advanced up the sidewalk. Unease washed through her. Then it struck her she could see the stars perfectly. The back light at the door wasn't on. And Mary hadn't opened the door as soon as she got to it like she usually did. Jamaica knocked hard and long. No one answered. *She just called me with an order less than an hour ago.* She pounded on the door, yelling, "Mary! Are you okay?" *She has one minute to open this door before I call 911. God I wish I had asked her where she hides the spare house key.*

The door opened, showing a sleep-eyed Mary. "Oh, Jamaica. I'm sorry I feel asleep watching the end of the movie. I forgot all about the ice cream order. Come in, dear." Mary shuffled away, leaving her to follow.

Jamaica's eyes narrowed; her brow furrowed as she followed Mary into the kitchen. "I brought everything you wanted. Shall I put the pint of maple walnut in the freezer for you?"

"Yes, please. That would be fine." Mary sat down at the table, slumping in her seat, rubbing her eyes.

After putting the ice cream in the freezer, she walked over to the table and sat down. "Are you okay, Mary? Do you feel all right?" She set the bag containing their sundaes on the table between them.

"I'm fine. I'm just tired." Mary rubbed her face. "Maybe you should put the sundae in the freezer too. I don't think I want to eat it now."

"Okay. I should probably leave so you can get to bed." Jamaica put Mary's sundae in the freezer. "As long as you're sure you're all right."

At the back door she turned around, the pit of her stomach heavy. "Good night, Mary."

"Wait." Mary called out. "Come here, Jamaica."

As instructed, Jamaica went back to the kitchen table.

Mary stood and reached out for her hand. "Do I detect something wrong? Why so sad tonight? What's happened?"

Jamaica hung her head, silent tears sliding down her face. "It's my mom's anniversary."

Giving Jamaica's hand a firm squeeze, Mary said, "I understand. How long has it been now?"

"Ten years this year." She sobbed outright, tears streaming down her face. "I can't—"

"It's okay." Mary enfolded her in her frail arms, letting Jamaica weep as long as it took. "You were so young when you lost her."

"I wasn't that young. Twenty-four."

Mary whispered softly. "Darling, twenty-four is so young. You still needed your mother. A woman always needs her mother, throughout her whole life."

"It's just hitting me harder today. I think Dad forgot what day it was. He didn't say anything about it this morning at breakfast and I didn't want to remind him."

"Hmm, I'm sure he didn't forget. He probably thought that same thing about you." Mary rubbed her back soothingly. "You two should talk about her. It will help with the grief."

Jamaica sniffed, "All I end up doing is crying when I start talking about her."

"But you remember her. And eventually, you'll remember all the good times and the hurt won't hurt quite so bad."

She shrugged. "Not likely."

"I didn't say it was going to be easy, or fast. It's never going to stop hurting entirely. But it does get a tiny bit easier each day to go on."

Jamaica nodded. She glanced over at the far wall in the living room, the wall of pictures. Mary still wore a thin wedding band, but Jamaica had never seen or heard her speak of a husband. And the pictures showed a male child, from babyhood to about high school age. "You know from experience too?"

"Yes. My husband died eight years ago. It was a heart attack at work. He worked construction. He kissed me goodbye one morning, picked up his lunch, and drove away. That was the last I saw him alive."

Her heart aching for her friend, Jamaica gave her a hug. "I'm so sorry. That must have been the worst."

Mary got up, shuffled into the kitchen, and poured a glass of water. She held it up to Jamaica, offering a drink. As Jamaica shook her head, Mary drained the glass then returned.

"No, losing Charlie wasn't the worst. That came before then. When Todd was killed." She sat down heavily at the table. "Bosnia. It was a peacekeeping mission. But land mines don't know when wars are over."

Jamaica recoiled, her gut dropping. "Oh, Mary. I'm so very sorry for your loss. Army?"

"Yes." Her arms resting on the table, Mary flashed her hands upwards. "What can you do? What can you say when they want to enlist and they're of age? All you can do is wish them well and pray every minute of every day until they return home."

The two women were silent for a minute, each lost in their own thoughts.

Mary's voice rose. "I focus on Celeste and her family now. She's all I have left." Then her head drooped.

"Let me help you to bed." Jamaica walked Mary to the bedroom, tucking her in under the goose-down comforter she used all year round. "Good night, Mary. I'll see you tomorrow."

"Good night, Jamaica." Mary grasped her hand and squeezed it. "You have a golden heart. You should have a family of your own. Hasn't anyone ever won your heart?"

Jamaica sat on the edge of the bed, clinging to Mary's hand. "Yes, once. A long time ago, back in high school someone set my heart afire with possibilities of marriage and a family. But it didn't work out." Tears seeped into her eyes as she remembered. "It hasn't happened again since then."

Mary smiled, her own eyes closed as her head rested on the pillow. "Hmm. I thought as much. I had a grammar school sweetheart. But he moved away."

"What was his name?" Jamaica teased.

"Oh, I don't remember after all these years. We're talking sixty-something years ago. But I remember his face. At least I still have that." Mary patted Jamaica's hand. "Get going home, you. And thank you for reminding me of my boys. It hurts but it's wonderful to remember them. They feel close again when I do."

CHAPTER FOURTEEN

The sky was blue with puffy white clouds scattered here and there as far as Jamaica could see. She walked a little faster, having decided at the last minute to post a check to the cellphone company. It was now five minutes to opening time. She walked past Kevin's store, opened since nine o'clock in the morning. It was deserted, even for a Saturday morning, when it should have been packed with customers.

Jamaica shook her head. Kevin was such a nice guy but such a lousy businessman. His store was small, dark, and kept rather dank. The cards he offered were off label or unfamiliar brands. Good cards, but not your standard American Greetings or Hallmark brands. And the gifts he offered for sale were not great. For someone in a hurry or needing a last-minute gift, his shop sufficed. But anyone with a car and enough time would head out of town to the nearest strip mall for better pickings.

As Jamaica walked past Ronnie's store, she saw no sign of him. It was after ten so he was open, though the place was deserted, or so it seemed from the street.

With the check posted, Jamaica headed back to her shop, hoping to get there before the eleven o'clock posted opening time. As she passed Ronnie's store, he flagged her over from his front window. She paused on the sidewalk, tempted to ignore his summons then decided to give him a few minutes of her time and see what he wanted. He met her at the door.

"Hey, I heard you made a possible identification." Ronnie said as soon as she stepped inside.

"Yeah, it was pretty freaky. I really didn't think it was going to work. They had me put an index card over the lower portion of each of the faces in the mug shots so I could concentrate strictly on the suspect's eyes. I knew those eyes as soon as I saw them." She rubbed the toe of her sneaker at a scuff mark on a white tile of Ronnie's floor. "It was kind of scary," Jamaica admitted.

"Well, I'm proud of you for doing it. It took guts, and I'm glad you found them."

Jamaica stood still and silent a few seconds. "What do you mean, glad I found some guts?"

"I didn't mean it like it sounded," Ronnie blurted out, turning beet red.

All the thoughts about missing supplies, her father's loan, her lack of proper sleep, and her fear of bankruptcy coalesced in a ball in the center of her chest and exploded. "I'll bet you did, Ronnie. Here we go again. High school all over again, is it? I've got guts. I've got a lot of guts. Maybe you didn't think so back then, and maybe you don't think so now, but I'm strong. And I don't need you or anyone else's help. I'm running that business across the street on my own. I don't need you or any man to try to tell me what I need to do."

"Jones, you didn't have any guts back in high school, and you barely have any today. Shit, it took my coaxing to get you to the police station to even look at those mug shots, didn't it? So, don't tell me you don't need anyone. Cuz, Jamaica, sometimes you can't get out of your own way even if it is for your own good." Ronnie got right into her face, his breath brushing her cheek.

Jamaica pulled away and stomped across the store. She flung up her hands. "Oh, here we go. Back in high school again. You'll never forgive me for turning you down for sex, will you, Ronnie? Did I bruise your ego so badly, that all these years later, you still can't get over the sight of me?" She too, got right into his face for the last sentence.

Ronnie pulled back. He prowled around the store as if looking for something. He walked behind the ice cream counter and glared at her. "Look Jamaica. I loved you. It didn't seem to matter to you. We were a couple. We had plans for the future. None of it mattered to you.

The only thing that mattered was your perfect virginity. Well, how is it today? Still protecting the citadel?"

Jamaica stood, eyes wide, mouth hung open, speechless. "I trusted you to understand. You didn't then and still don't today. Well, fine, just fine." She threw a stack of napkins at him behind the counter. "I don't need you, I don't need any man. You're all alike. You all want something I'm not willing to give up so easy. And I'm not willing to give up my business either so you and your store can go screw."

Why do we always end up fighting? Why do I always open my mouth, say the wrong thing, and set her off? Ronnie frowned, looking at Jamaica but not really hearing her as she ranted on. A stirring in his groin began as he watched her antics. *She really is gorgeous when she's all fired up.* Passion flared in her eyes, her hair slipped out of its fancy do, and her face flushed, he watched entranced by the sight of her. Until she noticed the front of his pants and her expression darkened even more.

He rubbed the back of his neck, shrugged and grimaced. Based on the reaction on Jamaica's face, she wasn't happy with his expression. This set her off again, raving about the treatment she had to endure in high school when he left her. He searched his brain for a way to defuse the situation. Clearly, nothing he said could stop her once she got going.

Ronnie glanced around the store, looking for something — anything that might interrupt and end the argument, one-sided though it might be at this point. He spotted the ice cream scoop. *Hell, why not. Maybe it will get her attention and shut her up.* Ronnie grabbed the handle, slid open the top of the ice cream freezer and scooped up a ball of the nearest flavor. Jamaica wasn't paying attention as she argued her point. Ronnie took aim and let it fly.

Splat!

A ball of ice cream hit the doorframe inches from Jamaica's head. She turned to look at Ronnie, whose hands held another glob of ice cream, ready for launch. He let it fly, Jamaica ducked in time, hearing

MELT MY HEART

the glob splat against the door window at a level where her head might have been.

Running to the other end of the ice cream freezer, Jamaica grabbed the nearest scoop and dug out a handful of ice cream, flinging the ball and hitting Ronnie square in the chest. He heaved a ball at her, hitting her in the side of the face, knocking her sunglasses off her head. Jamaica re-armed and threw a ball of chocolate at Ronnie's head. He ducked, the ball skidding across the floor. He dug out a huge ball of ice cream with the scoop and let it fly, except he lost his grip on the scoop too. Jamaica dodged it deftly, but the scoop and ice cream struck the plate glass window. They watched in horror as the tempered glass shattered into thousands of bits. People walking along the sidewalk stood stunned looking in at them.

Jamaica and Ronnie looked at each other. With the ball of ice cream in her hand, Jamaica let it fly. Gasps from outside seemed to echo through the interior of the shop. Ronnie snatched up another scoop and retaliated.

They continued throwing, getting hit, ducking, and missing. Then one of Ronnie's balls of ice cream went wide, and with another collective gasp from the huge crowd outside, it struck a police officer in the face.

A sharp, loud whistle pierced the air, stopping both of them, Jamaica's arms extended in windup. Two police officers stood just inside the door of the store and a couple dozen people outside the store watched through the open area where the window pane had been.

"Turn around with your hands up," one police officer called out. "Drop the —ah —"

"Scoops." Ronnie and Jamaica said in unison.

They did as they were told, dropping their scoops and handfuls of sticky ice cream, their hands numb and dripping. They were handcuffed and brought out to separate cruisers. The crowd murmured as they were led past them. Kevin Dailey asked, "Who won?"

***

Jamaica refused to do anything in the tiny cell but stand. By standing, the only direct contact she had with her surroundings was through her shod feet. *I won't need a reminder to burn these shoes when I leave this place.*

The gray cinder block walls of the cell had a perpetual grimy appearance, as though each of the last hundred occupants of the cell had smeared the walls with God-only-knew-what body fluid, then threw dirt at it. At least she hoped it was dirt. The equally gray floor wasn't much better though it did have remnants of a glossy shine in the corners, under all the dirt and dust bunnies. But no bunnies would choose to hang out here. These had to be dust moles or voles or some other dirt happy creature that would enjoy the filth.

Jamaica glanced at her watch but it wasn't on her wrist. Likewise, her belt and shoelaces had been taken away before she was directed into the cell. Except for the clothes on her own back and her lace-less shoes, there was nothing left. Even her jewelry had been taken away. How she might have hurt herself with her watch was beyond her imagination.

A closed-circuit camera spied her every movement, which wasn't much. She didn't want to risk touching anything. Bad enough she had to breathe the air in the cell. The smell of it alone was enough to gag anyone weaker of stomach. A volatile combination of sweat, stale beer, dirt, and vomit. It reeked, giving Jamaica another reason to breathe as shallowly as possible.

Down the corridor, Jamaica could hear a cop escorting Ronnie into a cell. She could hear him cursing as the door slammed shut. The shuffling sounds of feet and incoherent muttering echoed across the dark, dingy walls. A rattle sounded at times as he grabbed at the bars. She would give anything to be able to hear what he was saying.

The room held three cells. Each was identical to the others. Same gray cinder block walls, gray cement floor and a metal bench, the ends embedded into the wall. The gray metal bars were at least an inch in diameter and looked like they had come right out of an old, western movie set.

"Did you really have to start an ice cream fight?" she called to Ronnie, knowing he could hear her thirty feet away.

"Jam, don't start. Far as I'm concerned, this fight is over."

Jamaica continued, ignoring his statement. "I want to get this all out. You've hated me since I turned you down. I've hated you for walking out on me."

"That was years ago. Past. Done. Over. As the saying goes, let sleeping dogs lie, for Pete's sake. I'm over you, now get over yourself."

"Get over myself? I've been over you for so long that I'd almost forgotten what you looked like. You're one to talk. All of a sudden, you come back to town to ruin my business and ruin my life again." Jamaica paced the small cell, hands fisted at her side.

"I have as much right to come back here as you did. It just took me a little longer to return. And I didn't know you owned Mr. Nichol's ice cream shop. I never imagined you might own it." His voice gave a little echo as it bounced along the cinder block walls.

"How can you say that? All I talked about through high school was becoming a pastry chef. All I ever wanted was to have my own shop."

"I had no idea it was *you* behind the Emporium. That night at O'Toole's Tavern, when I was just back in town, I couldn't believe it when you told me you owned the shop. It was too late to change my plans. Too late to make changes without losing all my money."

"No, I don't believe it. And then you get back together with Brenda! Brenda, of all people! Shoot me, Ronnie. I mean, how can you possibly expect me to believe that wasn't planned either." Jamaica kicked the wall, then grimaced as her big toe began to ache.

"Brenda and I are not back together. I turned her down."

"You expect me to believe that after what I've seen with my own two eyes, in your front window? You were making out like there wasn't going to be another sunrise."

"She kissed me. It surprised me, I didn't know what hit me. I did not kiss her back."

"I'll bet." Jamaica stopped pacing and crossed her arms over her chest. "And you went out to dinner, did you not?"

"Well, yes, but that was just when I first got into town. I was hoping she'd leave me alone after that."

"Hmm. Right."

"Please, Jam. Let's forget it. Bury the hatchet, as they say."

"Yeah, right between your two eyes would be the perfect spot."

Ronnie groaned. Jamaica could hear footsteps retreating, before coming closer and closer, then retreating again.

He returned to the conversation. "Remember when you said, we should leave it up to the public to decide which ice cream store it liked best? I think we should continue in that manner."

"No." Jamaica snapped through clenched teeth.

Ronnie sighed. "Well, I'm not closing, and I don't expect you are either so we're at a stalemate."

The door at the end of the anteroom opened. Sergeant Alden came strolling in, a ring of keys in hand. He walked past Ronnie's cell over to Jamaica. "You still not going to press charges, is that correct, Ms. Jones?"

She shook her head slowly.

He walked over to Ronnie's cell. "And you, Mr. Caswell? Pressing charges?"

"No."

"Ladies first," He unlocked Jamaica's door and waved her to follow him.

They left the prisoner holding area, entering a side room near the front desk of the police station. There, waiting for her, was her father.

MELT MY HEART

Jamaica's heart leapt as she saw his gaunt face and frail body stooped over with age and arthritis. What remained of her anger toward Ronnie instantly dissolved into shame at having disrupted her father's comfort as well as embarrassed him.

"Daddy, I'm so sorry." She rushed over to give him a hug and kiss.

Sydney Jones gave his daughter as big a hug as he could muster. Then he looked her over, head to toe to assure himself she was okay. "Never thought I would ever see you in jail, young lady."

Jamaica cringed at the statement. Tears welled in her eyes and started to spill over. "I never intended this to happen, Daddy. I'm so very sorry," she cried.

He patted her back and stepped away.

Ronnie started to walk by the open door of the room they were in. He stopped and stepped inside. "Mr. Jones, I'm very sorry for having upset you with this episode."

"Ronald Caswell. Haven't seen you in a dog's age." Sydney Jones held out his hand.

"You and Jamaica were a thing once. You took good care of her. I respected you back then. This behavior now surprises me. I expect better from you."

He hung his head a few seconds before replying. "I know, sir. I'm sorry."

Mr. Jones looked from his daughter to Ronnie and back again. "Promise me this will never happen again."

Both agreed.

Ronnie left to get his things from another police officer. While Jamaica wiped tears from her cheeks with the back of her hand.

Sargent Alden waved Jamaica over to the table, placed a pen in her hand and showed her where to sign the release. He gave her a bag with her belongings and wished her a good day.

Jamaica put herself together, replacing her belt, shoelaces, and jewelry.

When they started out the door, Ronnie returned. "You two need a lift home?"

She looked at her father, her eyes big with surprise. "Oh my gosh Daddy, how did you even get here?"

"The next-door neighbor drove me over. I can call him."

Ronnie interjected. "Nonsense. I'll give you both a lift. Just wait a few minutes while I run over to get my car. It's behind the store."

Jamaica nodded. "You only have to drive us to my car behind my store. I can take my father home from there."

It was only a five-minute wait for Ronnie. They squished into the front cab of his pickup truck, Jamaica between the two men. The heat of Ronnie's thigh burning along her own. *How many times did we sit snuggled together like this during high school? Well, without my father as chaperone.*

Driving by Ronnie's shop, they were surprised to see the front window space was already boarded up with plywood.

"I wonder who did that." Ronnie said.

Jamaica shook her head. "If I had to guess, it would be Kevin's handiwork. Unless the building owner did it."

The pickup turned into the parking lot behind Jamaica's building. Sydney Jones got out of the vehicle. Before Jamaica could scooch out, Ronnie's hand stopped her. "I'm sorry for today."

Jamaica sighed. "Me too. I'm sorry."

"Let's try to not let it happen again." He tilted his head aside. "Deal?"

She smiled wearily. "Deal."

CHAPTER FIFTEEN

The letter came in the mail the next day. Jamaica read the letter several times before she understood what the president of the Merchants Association was intending to do.

Dear Ms. J. Jones,

A situation has been brought to my attention involving yourself and another merchant on Main Street. This situation has grown out of control and must be contained. For this reason, I am requesting your presence at a special, closed door meeting at the VFW hall, tomorrow evening, August 15th at 8PM for discussion and mediation.

Sincerely,

Benjamin Salters

President, Downtown Merchants Assoc.

"He wants to mediate the argument between Ronnie and myself. What a bloody fool!" Jamaica said aloud. Funny how he specifically chose the closing time of both their shops as the meeting time. *No getting around the summons from the big cheese.*

***

At five minutes after eight o'clock, the next day, Jamaica entered the VFW hall to find Ben Salters and Ronnie Caswell already seated at a small circular table. Salters had a Styrofoam cup of coffee with him, as did Ronnie. Jamaica wished she had thought well enough in advance to bring at least a bottle of water. She didn't think this meeting was going to be ending anytime soon.

"Ah, welcome Jamaica. So good of you to come," Salters said, setting down his coffee cup.

She walked over, flopped her handbag on the floor beside the one empty chair at the table and sat in it. "So nice of you to invite me." She tried to sound as sweet as she could without sounding too sarcastic.

"Right. Let's get started, shall we?" Salters folded his hands on the table in front of him. "I've been aware of the problems and issues passing between you two members of the Downtown Merchants Association since our last meeting. I understand things have escalated to the point of police involvement. Let me say, this is totally unacceptable. Besides being against the rules of this association, it is morally wrong. As merchants, we should be working to assist each other, uphold our standards of practice, and share in each other's successes. I don't see this happening between you two."

Jamaica cut Salters off, her palm over her heart, "Sir, I understand your concern, but you have to understand mine. I've purchased this wonderful business, renovated it, and have been working hard to build it into a success for the last five years. Now that it's almost able to stand on its own, along comes this upstart with a competing commodity." She hammered her index finger into the table top as she made each point.

"Upstart? I'm hardly an upstart. Fulton River is my hometown and where my grandparents' store was located. Naturally, I gravitated back here."

Benjamin Salters interjected, "But you had to have known, by driving through town, that the ice cream parlor that was here when you were a child, was in fact, still here, Mr. Caswell."

"Yes, I knew the Vermont Ice Cream Emporium was still here. But the ice cream I remember having there wasn't nearly as good as the stuff I planned to offer. So, I thought survival of the fittest," Ronnie explained. He took a sip from his coffee cup. His eyes never leaving Jamaica's face.

Benjamin Salters frowned. "You knowingly opened a competing business. Not what we in the association would call a judicious maneuver."

Jamaica stewed over her next move. Was it in her best interest to go for it? *To hell with it,* she thought. "It's not bad enough he's taking away customers and ruining my business, I have reason to believe he had something sinister to do with the robbery I suffered several weeks ago."

Both Benjamin Salters and Ronnie Caswell stared at her, open-mouthed at this pronouncement.

Remembering his role, Salters found his voice. "What exactly do you mean by that?"

Jamaica tapped the tabletop with each syllable she uttered to reinforce her point. "What I mean is, I have reason to believe Mr. Caswell was involved in my being robbed."

Ronnie stood so suddenly his chair went flying five feet behind him. "I resent that accusation. I had nothing, *nothing* at all to do with the robbery of Ms. Jones' shop."

Eyes narrowed, Jamaica sneered, "Really? That's not what the robber said! He made it pretty damn clear to me you were involved in sending him."

Still standing, hands on his hips, Ronnie shot back, "What did he say? This I need to hear. Whatever it was, it was a damn lie."

Jamaica rushed toward him, stopping to stand toe to toe with Ronnie. Benjamin Salters shifted in his chair before finally standing, perhaps in case he had to jump between them.

Anger flashed in Jamaica's eyes. "On his way out the back door, the man said, 'payback is a bitch.' I heard it loud and clear. And there's no one else I know of who wants to pay me back other than you, Ronnie." Her hands on her hips, her chest heaved.

Ronnie stared at her dumbfounded. "Payback is a bitch? Based on that phrase you assume I was involved in the robbery?" He let out a tense chuckle. Turned and started to pace the floor.

"You're the only person in the world who has anything against me."

He stopped and turned toward her. "I have nothing against you, Jamaica. I have no reason, no motive to seek payback."

"Then who else could possibly want payback from me?" Jamaica asked.

All three of them stood looking at each other.

Benjamin Salters was the first to blink. "Let's all sit down and think this through."

Jamaica slowly returned to her chair while Ronnie righted his own. Mr. Salters eyed them both before being the last to sit down.

Ronnie was the first to say anything. He scooched forward in his seat, spreading his hands on the table. "Let me get this straight. The robber comes in, puts a gun to your head and asks for money. Correct?"

Jamaica nodded.

"You give it to him and he bolts out the back door saying, 'Payback is a bitch?'"

"Yes," Jamaica acknowledged.

All was silent as they thought this through.

Ronnie again spoke first. "You were able to find a mug shot of the perp, correct?"

"Yeah, and from what the detective said, the finger prints match the escaped felon I picked."

"Gary Standler?" Ronnie leaned forward, waiting for a reply.

"How did you know?" Jamaica's mouth hung open.

Blood drained from Ronnie's face as his eyes went wide. "Are you sure?"

Jamaica's eyes went wide watching Ronnie's response as she realized something was terribly amiss, "Yeah, completely."

Flopping in his chair, Ronnie voice rose in pitch, "That's the guy who shot me. I heard he was out, but I didn't think he was stupid enough to come after me again."

Ronnie was silent again for a few seconds before bursting out in such a loud voice he scared Jamaica and Benjamin Salters. "He was trying to rob *me*."

"What?" both Jamaica and Salters said in unison.

"Gary Standler was involved in an attempted armed robbery. I was involved in capturing him, and in the process took one of his bullets.

For both those reasons, he was sentenced to fifteen years in prison. He escaped a couple weeks ago. He's probably coming after me for putting him away."

"Why didn't he go to your store? Why did he come to mine?" Jamaica leaned forward in her chair.

"Maybe he thought he was in my store."

Benjamin Salters interrupted. "This is great. We've established the robber's potential motive and cleared the air about who was and wasn't involved with him." He gloated sitting with his shoulders back and head held high as if balancing a crown.

Both Jamaica and Ronnie looked at each other and nodded in agreement.

Salters continued, "So we're back to the only contention being the deliberate opening of a store offering competing products."

Ronnie stood and began pacing. "Look, I didn't know Jamaica owned the Emporium. I wanted to reopen my grandparents' store. I've wanted to work in that store since I was a kid. And the time was right." He pressed a palm to his forehead and then spun around. "Let's let the public decide which ice cream they prefer."

Jamaica rose to the bait. "What are you proposing? Because the problem is, while the public is deciding, I'm going bankrupt. By the time they decide who the winner is, it may be too late to make a choice. I don't know about you, Ronnie, but I can't go on indefinitely."

Ronnie came to stand between Salters and Jamaica. He leaned on the back of his chair, "I'm not sure what I'm proposing." He scrubbed his hand through his hair. "I can't go on much longer either."

Salters asked, "What's the solution?"

"We need the people of this town to make up their minds faster," Jamaica said.

The three of them were silent again. Ronnie sat down in his chair.

"I've got it," Salters interjected. "Why not have an actual competition? I propose your two shops go head-to-head for title of the best ice cream in Fulton River at the festival."

Ronnie and Jamaica stared at Salters, then at each other. The festival was two weeks away. A cold shiver ran down Jamaica's spine. As much as she wanted the situation resolved soon, did she really want it resolved so soon?

Ronnie spoke up first. "Let me get this straight. Jamaica and I compete for best ice cream in Fulton River, and the winner, wins what exactly?"

Salters smiled. "It's not so much what the winner wins, it's what the loser loses. The loser loses the right to sell ice cream in the town of Fulton River."

"But if by some miracle Ronnie wins, that would put me completely out of business!"

"Well, the way I see it, you could change your business plan. Become something else. A bakery or a tea shop or anything unrelated to ice cream. If you lose," Salters said. "And if Caswell loses, he becomes just a candy store, for example."

Ronnie and Jamaica looked at each other again.

Anxious for a resolution, Salters pushed the issue. "Come on. Let's see you two shake on this idea. The Merchants Association will come up with the rules and do the advertising for the event so everyone in town will be aware of the competition and its consequences."

The two adversaries stared at each other, Jamaica biting her lower lip but remaining silent. *It's my baby, my life, my career. Should I bet its future like a game of chance at the fair*?

"I'm game." Ronnie held out his right hand to Jamaica. "A quick answer beats a slow death and bankruptcy for both of us."

Jamaica's knees shook and a thick lump formed in her throat at the thought. But she had to admit, it was a fair and easy means of settling the controversy. She knew she had the better ice cream. This would

MELT MY HEART

prove it to everyone, once and for all. And stop the slow financial bleeding of her store.

She took Ronnie's hand and shook it.

CHAPTER SIXTEEN

Jamaica and Ronnie stood on the sidewalk outside the VFW. Her stomach growling loudly reminded her she hadn't eaten dinner yet. Jamaica looked at her watch. It was almost nine o'clock.

"You sound hungry," Ronnie swayed back and forth on his heels. "I assume you didn't have dinner before the meeting, either?"

Jamaica shook her head. "No, no time. I had things to make for tomorrow."

"Look, let me take you to the diner. It's not far, just over in Townshend. They have great food. I know you'll like it." He half turned, one arm extended, as though inviting her to walk off with him.

She shook her head. "Thanks, but I have some soup back in the shop." She toed the sidewalk crack, before adding, "you're welcome to join me if you'd like."

He looked at her, his head tilted. "Sure, why not. Can you make a cup of coffee too?"

"I can do better than that. I have a bottle of wine, some cheese, and homemade bread to go with it." Jamaica smiled. It was odd getting to know this adult Ronnie. The Ronnie she last knew was seventeen and more interested in eating pizza with a contraband beer. He seemed like a total stranger now. Except he wasn't. She wondered how much of the old Ronnie Caswell was still lurking there, under his skin.

"Wine sounds great, as does the bread. Let's go."

They met up at her shop, entering the store through the back door. Jamaica gathered the goods: the cheese, bread, butter, wine, and glasses. Ronnie took each from her and placed them on the old farmers table tucked in a corner of her kitchen. Jamaica heated up the pasta e fagioli soup while Ronnie opened the bottle of wine and poured each of them a glass.

"This is kind of a heavy soup for so late in the evening, but it is hearty."

MELT MY HEART

"We'll just have to stay up late to let it settle." Ronnie carried both glasses over to Jamaica, at the stove. He handed her a glass and proposed a toast. "To ice cream, in all its delicious flavors."

"Cheers." Jamaica clinked her glass with Ronnie's glass. They both sipped the Sangiovese. "God, this is going to taste great with the soup." She stirred the contents of the pot again to prevent burning.

Ronnie leaned against the other end of the stove. "You know, I've been thinking about all the good times we had. The memories keep coming back to me."

Jamaica was unable to help but smile at the statement. She ladled out the soup into two white crocks, then carried them over to the table. Ronnie followed carrying both glasses of wine. They sat down and started to eat the soup.

"Ah, Jam, this is great soup. Did you make the bread too?" At her nod he said, "You should put this on the menu."

"Can't, it's an ice cream shop," she resumed blowing on her spoonful of soup.

Ronnie set down his spoon and began slicing the loaf of homemade bread. He handed a slice to Jamaica, who slathered it with butter. "So, what do you remember most from our days at Fulton River High School?"

Jamaica chewed her bread for a minute, swallowed, and placed the slice down beside her crock. "I think what I remember most is the day after prom. We all went out to Townsend State Park and spent the day. It was beautiful and so much fun with all our friends."

"Yeah, that's right up there for me too."

They both took a spoonful of soup, eyes downcast.

After swallowing Jamaica asked, "What was the most memorable day for you?"

Ronnie cocked his head to the side and smiled. "I have to say, prom was special. You looked beautiful in that red gown. You should have been prom queen."

Jamaica laughed at the thought. How could Ronnie have remembered her dress was red after all these years? And prom queen, instead of Melody Haines? True, Melody might have been beautiful, but she didn't have two cents worth of common sense to her name. "What about you? You should have been prom king. Your tux was perfect for you. You looked so handsome," she said wistfully.

They continued to eat their soup, sopping up the last of the broth with a slice of bread.

"That was good. Thanks, Jam."

"I'm glad you liked it. Sure beats a drive to the diner at this hour of the night."

Ronnie poured each of them another glass of wine. "You know what I think most about?"

"What's that?"

"How well we got along together during those days. We never fought. We never bickered like other couples did. Why do you figure that was? Were we so attuned to each other that we were equally matched or was it something else?"

"I don't know." Jamaica fingered the stem of her wineglass, in thought. "We were well matched. We liked to do the same things. And if we didn't, we still supported each other. Like you were captain of the swim team, and I'd be there to cheer you on. And when I was in marching band, you were always on the sidelines cheering me on during football half time and at parades. That kind of support is hard to find these days, isn't it?"

"Sure is."

"And you tried so hard to get into the Coast Guard but were rejected. We both cried together over that." Jamaica held her fist up to her lips and swallowed hard.

"Yeah, all those high school summers being a lifeguard, I was sure would be a help getting in and they didn't." He smiled. "But I had to be a lifeguard, because you couldn't swim. Did you ever learn?"

Jamaica shook her head. "Never learned. It's not high on my priority list."

They were silent again for a few minutes, sipping their wine. Jamaica got up and walked over to the couch. The wine was making her bold, she waved Ronnie over. He followed.

"You have much luck with women?" Jamaica asked, sipping at her wine, keeping her eyes lowered.

Ronnie paused, glass midway to his mouth. He put his arm down. "No. I mean, I've had girlfriends, but nothing ever seemed to click. Not like us." He took a gulp of wine and swallowed hard. "And you?"

Jamaica twirled her wineglass. "No, not many. They usually are around for a couple dates, then they leave. I, eh, have a tendency to turn down their offers for sex. It doesn't seem right after the second or third date. I need to know someone better."

Ronnie watched as Jamaica blushed crimson. A small smile appeared on his face, as if that buoyed his spirits. "You were better off without them."

He topped off each of their glasses.

"Yeah, I know. But it was sort of déjà vu." She looked away, wishing to hide the welling tears in her eyes.

Now, Ronnie felt the heat of his blush. *She's right of course.* He had done no better their senior year in high school. Suddenly, he became angry. Angry with his teenage self for doing that to Jamaica. She had done nothing to warrant such treatment. She had deserved his love and respect and he had bailed on her when she refused him.

He gently took her chin in his hand and turned her to face him. "I'm sorry, Jam. I'm so, so sorry," he said, staring into her eyes. "Please, can you ever forgive me?"

Tears started to roll down Jamaica's cheeks.

His heart heavy with the pain he caused her, Ronnie put his arms around her and pulled her to his chest, holding her close and rocking her as she cried. When she stirred, he kissed her tears, then her cheeks, then her eyes.

Jamaica's breath hitched, then sighed. Turning her head, her own lips quivered beneath his as her body did the same in his arms.

They kissed lightly at first. He deepened the kiss, opening her mouth and sliding his tongue inside. Their tongues touched and played. She tasted of the wine and the soup; rich and luscious.

Ronnie groaned deep in his throat as Jamaica's kisses became more insistent. He reclined back on the couch, pulling her on top of him. Jamaica made a little squealing noise. He released his hold. He feared she would sit up, putting an end to their encounter. He didn't want it to end. Ever. But he also knew every move would have to be hers…he would follow.

***

Sweet Jesus, I can't get him close enough. Jamaica grabbed a handful of his shirt and pulled him toward her, reversing their positions. Wrapping her legs around his, she wished she could melt into him.

Her heart swelled in her chest and burst open with love. Love that had been waiting all these years for Ronnie. Love she couldn't deny or hide or put off. He was here, now, and she wanted him back with every fiber of her body and soul. And this time, in this moment, she wasn't afraid.

Her hands wandered Ronnie's back, before moving up to his neck and pulling him into a deeper kiss. Then she pulled out of his embrace. Her hands meandered down over the taut muscles of his upper arms. One hand slid over to his hard chest. She wanted to cradle her head there again, as she had when she cried. But her hands kept up their exploration. He felt so good, every inch she touched led her on.

She looked up into Ronnie's face, saw his eyes had darkened. His skin. The need to be skin to skin with him overwhelmed her senses.

MELT MY HEART

Jamaica reached to unbutton her blouse, but Ronnie's hand stopped her. His eyes were bright and gleaming.

"Are you sure?"

Her eyes never leaving his, Jamaica brushed his hand off with trembling fingers and continued unbuttoning her blouse. "Yes, Ronnie. I'm sure."

He sat up, giving her space to move. Staring as Jamaica opened her top, he helped her slide out of it. She hoped her purple lace bra left enough to the imagination to drive him crazy with wonder at how she would look without it. He reached for the clasp but Jamaica met his lips and resumed kissing him, distracting him.

Ronnie reached up, cupping her breast with one hand, his thumb stroking her erect nipple. Jamaica moaned, her hands exploring up and down his chest and arms again. "Your shirt."

Dropping his lips to her neck, Ronnie began a trail of kisses from her ear to her shoulder. Louder moans broke from her lips when his tongue stroked the curve of her neck. "Your shirt."

"Mmm." Rubbing both nipples with his thumbs, his lips continued their search. His kisses spreading down her arm to her elbow, then crossing to her chest, leaving a flurry of kisses along the top of her bra.

Her breath ragged, and her heartbeat thrumming, Jamaica's hand slipped down to his hip and his buttocks, troking and kneading. The feeling of him inflamed her even more, spurring her on.

A sharp hiss escaped her lips as Ronnie's tongue made contact with a lace-covered nipple. On fire, she sank against him, forcing her nipple more firmly to his lips. He obliged, taking the hard peak between his lips and nibbling gently.

Her hand settled on the long hardness in his trousers. The firmness caused an aching and a wetness between her legs. An urgency filled her body. Her mind railed. There were too many impediments between them.

Nudging Ronnie away, she stood and shimmied out of her skirt and slip. The heat of a blush on her face, she stood in front of him in her panties and bra, her arms held awkwardly over her chest.

"Undress me." Ronnie whispered.

Wide-eyed, she took Ronnie's hand and helped him to stand. Slowly, her eyes never leaving his, she began to undress him. First, removing his Oxford shirt, then his belt. At last she opened his trousers, letting them drop to the floor. Ronnie reached down into his back pants pocket and extracted a wrapped condom from his wallet.

They stared at each other. Jamaica in her matching bra and French cut panties; Ronnie in his briefs. He opened his arms and Jamaica stepped into them, engulfed in the warmth and softness of his skin.

Ronnie guided her to lie down on the couch before following so they lay side by side. Their lips met again, the fire burning brighter and deeper this time. Hands roamed, touching here, exploring there. The heat building in him until they had to break their kiss because of their panting.

Ronnie unclasped Jamaica's bra, pulling it aside, out of his way. Her nipples, free of the lacy warmth, hardened further. His tongue searched out one, then the other nipple, laving each as Jamaica groaned, her fingers were grasping Ronnie's head, pulling him closer to suckle her nipples, as his tongue played with each. His hands, full of her breasts, kneaded and caressed in time with his tongue. Glorying in the beauty of them, he confessed, "My God, Jam. Your breasts are so beautiful. I could caress them all day long."

He smiled at her surprise, then turned his attention back to kissing Jamaica's lips. Their tongues swirled and lips parted. He felt her hands wandering down his chest to his erection. His member responded, twitching hard at her touch. Stiffer than he had ever been in his entire life, he knew he wouldn't hold out if she handled him for long.

"I need you, now," she groaned, working off her panties.

"I thought you'd never ask." Ronnie chuckled softly. His hand drifted down her side, then his fingers slid to the apex of her thighs, finding wetness.

He doffed his briefs, ripped open the packet and donned the condom swiftly. She pulled him closer, his erection sinking into the junction of her legs. He slid back and forth slowly, teasingly, hoping to drive her crazy.

"Please Ronnie." Her arms reached for him.

Ronnie ran his hands along the outsides of her thighs, then parted her legs. His tip hit a barrier of the wellhead. He froze, pulling back as sweat broke out on his brow.

"No, you couldn't have waited." He remained still, his body tense, dizzy but unable to breathe, unable to think.

She pulled him toward her pleading, "Don't stop."

Exhaling sharply, he relaxed, gathered his breath and thoughts. Gently, he eased his way into the channel no man had previously entered. Jamaica's breath hitched as he slid inside, then she moaned and stilled.

Ronnie stopped. "Are you okay? Shall we quit?"

"Don't you dare stop now." She arched up against him, taking him deeper.

Her action nearly undid him. Her tightness, her wetness engulfed him as he thrust as gently and slowly as he could. Reaching down and finding her hard nub, he rubbed it lightly, causing Jamaica's moaning to increase. Continuing to rub and thrust until Jamaica was panting and writhing beneath him, he increased his pace, taking Jamaica over the edge to a shattering experience. As she came, he let go and quickly followed, as the spasms of her orgasm gripped him.

He wrapped his arms around her trembling body, pulled the afghan off the back of the couch, draping it over the two of them. They cuddled together under the warmth of the coverlet and the warmth of their lovemaking.

The ringing seemed far off, but she knew it was her cellphone's morning alarm. She opened her eye, finding herself in the arms of Ronnie Caswell. Moreover, she was naked, snuggled against his naked form, under the afghan.

Afraid to wake him, she lay still, praying the alarm would snooze itself after ten rings, as usual. It did but it was still too late.

Blue-green eyes met hers. "Good morning," he said.

CHAPTER SEVENTEEN

If she wasn't the one doing it, the humming would have driven her crazy. As it was, she couldn't stop it. It was out of the ordinary and totally out of character. But so was what happened last night.

Ronnie had graciously left shortly after waking up. No good morning kisses, no promises, no recriminations. Jamaica was grateful. Despite having been the instigator of the incident, in the light of day, and sober, she wasn't all together sure she had done the right thing.

She'd wanted to kiss him again. Especially after seeing how handsome he'd become as an adult. As she had grown older, she had always wondered what it might have been like to actually have said yes to his proposition all those years ago. Granted, he's probably a much better lover today than he must have been at seventeen. He must have had plenty of practice over the last twelve years. And despite her wavering sentiment on the memory of the event, she couldn't help humming. A warmth filled her chest making her feel happy, almost giddy.

Jamaica went about her morning, making a frozen almond raspberry dacquoise and a frozen chocolate peanut butter pie, two new menu items for the shop. They wouldn't be frozen in time to serve today but they would be ready for tomorrow. She had meant to make them after the meeting with Salters and Ronnie, last night, but, well, other wonderous things had happened instead.

As she made the peanut butter layer for the pie, Jamaica mused over the sudden turn of events. So much had taken place in just a couple hours' time. How Ronnie had figured out who the target of the robbery was meant to be, and how an impromptu dinner had led to a resumption of their relationship. Had it really, or was it wishful thinking on Jamaica's part? And what would this do to the upcoming ice cream war at the Fulton River Festival? Was it still on now?

Making love to Ronnie had opened the proverbial can of worms. Jamaica shook her head in disbelief. Too much to think about now. There were so many confusing emotions. She turned her focus back to the recipe she had devised and went to work on constructing the peanut butter pie.

Whining at the backdoor screen stopped her. She didn't have to look up to know it was Burpy. "You're back," she said. She walked over to the door and let the dog inside before going to fill his dog bowls. "You know, Burpy, you should stick around more often, instead of wandering the streets all the time. I might even want to adopt you full time if things work out here." Burpy didn't appear to be listening as he glared at her filling his kibble and water bowls and set them in their usual places beside his blanket. He gobbled the food down before slurping up all the water. After his usual three turns on the blanket and loud burp, he settled down and closed his eyes.

Jamaica sighed. Perhaps Burpy would never be tamed enough to stay. But Burpy needed her. What would happen to him if she had to close the business? She couldn't take him to her father's apartment if she moved out of her own apartment. He was allergic to cats and dogs. Who would take care of him? Who would feed him? Clearly no one else was doing it.

Her alarm went off, signaling that opening time drew near. Jamaica washed up at the hand sink. As she approached the front door to the shop, she couldn't help but look over at Ronnie's storefront. There on the front stoop was Brenda Tardash, having a few words with Ronnie. They seemed to be having a pleasant conversation. As they concluded their talk, Brenda placed her hand on Ronnie's forearm, leaned in and kissed him! On the lips!

Jamaica stepped away from the window, stunned. Here's the guy she slept with last night, gave her long-held virginity to, and he kisses that slut, Brenda Tardash, the next morning? *What the hell is he thinking?* Jamaica looked around for something, anything, to throw.

MELT MY HEART

There was nothing at hand. She kicked the nearest chair across the room instead.

And what the hell was I thinking? Did I really think things had changed between Ronnie and me? The answer is yes, damn it, I did. He sounded so convincing in that jail cell. If she faced the aching in her heart, she'd have to admit she loved him. That was what buoyed her mood all morning. The feeling of love. Of being loved and being in love. *Fool!* She was a fool to think things had changed for him as well as for her. Now she realized he was being male. Just another male out to see and take whatever female pleasures were offered. She banged the side of her head with her palm. With the door unlocked and "OPEN" sign turned outward, she righted the chair. Walking back to the kitchen area, she picked up the broom and started beating on the couch with the handle.

In several minutes, sweat was forming on her body and her arms ached. After her heart sank with jealousy and raged with indignation, it went light and airy. It was like having an umbrella when it starts to rain. Jamaica could feel the other emotions leach out of her like red dye in a new shirt. She didn't have to trust Ronnie. She didn't have to go out on a limb…the limb had already broken off.

She went back to work. There was no more humming.

The doorbell tinkling brought Jamaica out to the front room twenty minutes later.

It was Brenda. Better put away the broom.

"Hey Jamaica! How are you today?" she asked, her voice and step full of pep as she walked across the room to the counter.

"Fine Brenda. What will you have today?" Waiting on Brenda Tardash was the last thing on earth she wanted to do. No, correction. Waiting on Brenda was the second to last. The last person would be Ronnie Caswell.

"Oh, it's too early for ice cream and I have to watch my figure." She slid her hand down her side to accentuate her curves. "I came in to talk about the ice cream war I heard about from Ronnie. It's so exciting! I can't wait." She bent over the counter. "What flavors of ice cream are you going to be offering?" she added in a whisper, as though it was top secret.

Jamaica frowned, "Well, the Merchants Association is supposed to provide a list of rules. Until then, I have no idea how many flavors I can offer. So, I really can't tell you, Brenda." *Not that I would tell you anyway. You'll just run to Ronnie with the news.*

"Oh, I didn't know that. Ronnie didn't tell me that," Brenda giggled. "What a guy! He always forgets to tell me the details. Somehow, he seems to forget them whenever I'm around." She batted her eyelashes at Jamaica, and cocked her head to the side in an innocent manner.

"Maybe he didn't think it was any of your business." Jamaica folded her arms across her chest and leaned against the freezer cases.

The doorbell tinkled again. Both women looked up as Kevin Dailey entered.

"Hey Kevin, you're here early today. What's going on?" Jamaica asked.

"I just heard about an emergency meeting of the Merchants Association this afternoon at two. I was wondering if you were going?" he asked, approaching the women.

"I didn't hear about it, but if the topic is what I think it is, I shouldn't be in attendance anyway." Jamaica went on to explain the situation brewing and the Merchants Association involvement. Brenda stood, listening.

"Wow! Let me get this straight. You two are betting your ice cream businesses on a one-time public voting event? Are you crazy, Jam? This shop is your whole life. What are you going to do if you don't win?" Kevin asked.

Shrugging, Jamaica said, "I don't know, I don't plan to lose." *I only hope I manage to make enough money at the festival to cover the last of my expenses and pay back my Dad the money I owe him.*

"I wasn't going to go to the meeting, my store and all. But considering the ramifications, I'm going to close the store and attend. I don't want any funny business with this list."

"Thanks, Kevin. I appreciate it."

Kevin waved goodbye and left the shop.

Jamaica turned to stare daggers at Brenda, hoping she'd be the next one out the door.

Brenda didn't budge.

"Well, if you don't want any ice cream, perhaps you'll excuse me. I have some bookkeeping to do."

"Actually, I wanted to tell you something else." Brenda folded her hands together over her heart.

"What is it, now?" Jamaica began inspecting her fingernails.

"Ronnie and I are dating again. I know you had feelings for him back in high school and I thought just in case you still did, perhaps I should let you know, he's spoken for now."

"Really." Jamaica said flatly. "You sure about that?"

"Yes, of course. I just came from his store. Collected my morning kiss since we didn't stay together last night." She winked.

"Hmm, wonder where he was?" Jamaica goaded, then changed tactic. "I see. Well, thanks for telling me, but it wasn't necessary. He's all yours, Brenda." Jamaica picked up the nearest dish towel and flicked it at an imaginary fly. She missed.

"I knew you would understand." She smiled ear to ear and bounced up on the balls of her feet. "Well, got to go. Ta!" Brenda Tardash waltzed out of Jamaica's shop.

Jamaica viewed her shapely back end shimmy out the doorway.

***

Around six-thirty in the evening, Benjamin Salters came into the Emporium, interrupting Jamaica's dinner of grilled cheese and tomato soup. In his hand, he carried a manila folder of papers.

"I'm sorry to interrupt your dinner. I've brought the list of rules for the ice cream competition at the festival. The Merchants Association worked very hard on this, this afternoon. We feel the rules will provide a fair playing field for both contestants and give the public the opportunity to make the best choice."

Jamaica took the papers from Salters and read the rules aloud.

1. Any price may be set by the contestants.
2. No ice cream may be given away free of charge.
3. No offers may be made for a vote in exchange for money or goods of any kind.
4. Ice cream may be offered in either a dessert cup, a sugar cone, or cake cone.
5. The contestants may only offer up the following flavors: vanilla, strawberry, chocolate, coffee, and maple walnut.
6. No other products may be offered during the time of the tasting.
7. The winner will receive the "Best Ice Cream in Fulton River" award.
8. The loser will be required to immediately cease the sale of ice cream in Fulton River.
9. Both parties entering into the tasting must sign the contract stating they will abide by the rules thus presented.
10. Voting will be done by paper ballot. Voters, once having cast a ballot will have their left hand stamped with indelible ink.
11. No voter will be allowed to cast more than one ballot.
12. Votes will be counted by the head librarian of the Fulton River Public Library.
13. Any and all decisions are final.

"Give me the contract and a pen." Jamaica took the offered contract, signed above her typewritten name, and handed both to Mr. Salters.

"My, that was fast. You sure you don't have any questions or concerns?" Salters asked.

"My only concern is that you guys won't shut Caswell's ice cream operation down fast enough to suit me after I win the competition," Jamaica said, staring him squarely in the eyes.

"I'm on my way to his store now for his signature. I'll provide you both with a copy of the contract once he signs it."

"Great. I'll have it framed after I win," Jamaica quipped dryly.

Mr. Salters, not knowing what else to say, smiled warily, turned, and left.

Her back remained stiff until Mr. Salters was out the door and gone from her view down the street. Jamaica returned to the kitchen of her shop, shoulders slumped and head down. *If only I were as confident as I seem. I know my ice cream is great. But the public can be so fickle. The women may vote for Ronnie because he's handsome.*

There was no getting around it now. She would have to present her five flavors of ice cream, as they were, unadulterated with toppings and sauces. Not even a shot of real whipped cream. While Jamaica knew her ice cream was great, she also knew it was the sauces and toppings that made it outstanding. Could it beat Ronnie's ice cream? Or would she lose her shop, her career, her livelihood?

Jamaica threw out the remains of her sandwich and soup. She no longer had the appetite for either. Instead, she picked out a large bowl, take a scoop of each of the five flavors and taste tested them herself to ease her worries.

CHAPTER EIGHTEEN

Jamaica scribbled the sum in her business checkbook. *Minus two thousand, sixty-four dollars and seventeen cents.* Six, five-gallon tubs of each of the ice cream flavors came to over three thousand dollars. She was going to have to empty out her personal savings account to cover the bill. *There goes most of my money cushion. This really is a win or lose it all situation.*

The flying checkbook hit the back wall above the couch. The couch. She was going to have to do something about the couch. It was great to have for a quick nap before opening or to put her feet up if business was slow. But it had changed. An aura surrounded it now, making it incriminating. Jamaica didn't dare sit on it anymore.

The doorbell tinkled. A ruckus of giggling children spread throughout the shop. Jamaica smiled as she recognized the voices...Sara and Zachary Dailey, Kevin's children.

Rounding the archway into the front room, she was accosted by the two Dailey children, both trying to tickle her. Jamaica immediately went on the offensive, jutting out a tickling hand to Zachary. Her other hand snagged young Sara, scooping the child toward herself for a hug. Laughter erupted from her as they continued to attack her, their small hands doing more poking and pinching than tickling.

"Kids! Kids!" a pretty, brunette called. Madelaine Dailey, Kevin's wife, was of medium height but maximum presence. The former French teacher had kind eyes, and a generous mouth, which smiled constantly.

The girls ran back to their mother and father, leaving Jamaica to straighten out her apron.

"Ah, they're fine," Jamaica said, a little disappointed their fun had stopped.

But Maddie and Kevin's children were well behaved and listened to their parents, unlike most of the children who came into her shop. *How they manage two businesses and two children is beyond me!*

MELT MY HEART

Kevin's Cards and Gifts Store was next door and was his realm. He ruled it with a light hand. His wife, Maddie, on the other hand, ruled her photography studio like a ship on rough seas. She was one hundred percent at the helm, giving it the attention it needed to succeed.

And succeed it did. It was the best photography studio in a fifty-mile radius, the next closest competitor being in Montpelier. Her work, especially with children, was sought after by everyone in the area. Many expecting parents called to make appointments long before their baby's due date, just to be sure to get their newborn in for sensational photos.

Jamaica always left Maddie's presence hopeful and yet sad. Madelaine Dailey was everything Jamaica wished for herself. A successful businesswoman, a loving wife, and a doting, attentive mother.

"How are you all, today?" Jamaica bent over to the children's eye level.

The kids answered in unison, "Good, Miss Jamaica."

"That's good to hear! So what flavor are each of you having today?"

Kevin stepped in at this point. "Cones or cups, no sundaes today."

"Oh, Daddy!" five-year-old Zachary whined. "Why can't we have sundaes today?"

"Because your father said no." Maddie repeated, her voice on the stern side.

It was fifteen minutes before Jamaica got all the orders and another five for her to scoop and serve the ice cream. All the while, Maddie, Kevin, and Jamaica discussed the upcoming Fulton River Festival.

"I can't believe you are laying your business on the line over a taste test." Maddie shook her head and blinked rapidly. "The public can be so fickle. They might vote for Ronnie because you ran out of napkins in the napkin holder last time they visited."

"I know, but it is the only way to settle this once and for all. Business has been down and if it continues this way for much longer, great ice cream or not, I could go belly up. Better to do this now than string it out for another couple of months." Jamaica laid a hand on her cheek, then slid it to cover her mouth.

Kevin added, while wiping up spilled ice cream drips off the floor, "I thought your business was doing great?"

"It was doing great until Caswell came into town. I swear half the women in town go to his shop just to see his face. I'm left with the kids and the older folks."

Maddie looked at her and smiled. "You better hope those same women don't vote based on the looks of the proprietor instead of the flavor of the ice cream."

"I know. Well, good news is, the only way to get a ballot is to buy an ice cream. Essentially, only those tasting the ice cream get to vote." Jamaica smiled as she helped Sara wipe her face.

A cellphone trilled. Jamaica, expecting it to be Mary with an order, walked over to the counter and picked it up.

"Hello?"

"Hello, I'm looking for Miss Jamaica Jones, please," a woman said.

"Speaking." Jamaica nestled the cellphone closer to her ear.

"My name is Claire Boswell. I'm a nurse at the Brattleboro General Hospital Emergency Department. Your father was brought in by ambulance after a fall at home. He's not seriously injured but we do need you to come to the hospital to pick him up when we're finished casting his arm."

"Casting his arm? Did he break it? Is he all right?" Jamaica asked, her words coming quickly and impatiently.

"He has a hairline fracture in his left wrist. Nothing too serious but it is being put in a cast. Otherwise, he's doing fine. There was no dizziness or loss of consciousness. Apparently, he tripped over a jacket that fell on the floor," she said. "Also, when you're here, we would like to have the social worker talk with you about your father's situation. Perhaps there are resources available to help in his circumstances."

MELT MY HEART

"Okay, it's going to take me about an hour to get there, but I'm on my way."

"Thank you. See you soon," said Nurse Boswell before she hung up.

Returning to the front area, Jamaica saw the children had finished their ice cream and their faces had been cleaned by their parents. "It was the hospital. My father's in the emergency department. Tripped and broke his wrist. I have to go pick him up." Wringing her hands, Jamaica began removing her apron.

"Oh, gosh, Jam. Is there anything we can do to help?" Maddie asked.

"No, thanks. I'm going to have to close the shop while I'm gone and reopen if I can come back later."

The Dailey family said their goodbyes and left.

Jamaica scurried after them to turn the sign to "CLOSED" and locked the front door. In minutes, she was in her car and heading south on Route 91, toward Brattleboro.

***

Three hours later, Jamaica was back at her shop to reopen. It was six o'clock but there might still be some customers after the evening meal hours. Hopefully she could make a little more money before the end of the day.

Her father had been appropriately chastised for tripping over a jacket he had thrown onto the floor himself. The social worker and Jamaica had put their heads together to make sure he was getting all the community and nursing resources available to him. With the new injury, the visiting nurses would be coming in more often and the insurance would pay for daily, home healthcare aides.

It was a relief to Jamaica to know more help was available. It would help tide him over, making his own funds last longer. And it relieved Jamaica of some of the stress of helping him. Until the Fulton River Festival was over, she was going to be occupied with work.

The apron resettled about her waist, Jamaica went to work. Her to-do list for the evening was small, mainly dealing with checking inventory. She needed to make sure she would have enough sugar cones and dessert cups for the tasting event. Everything else was in adequate supply.

After checking the supply shelves, Jamaica was satisfied she would have enough stock for the festival. She sat down at her little table, suddenly famished. Her stomach reminded her she had not eaten since breakfast. A bowl of soup would fix the problem.

But as Jamaica opened the freezer door, a container of the same pasta e fagioli she had shared with Ronnie the other day stood out on the shelf. She lost her appetite. Shutting the freezer, she leaned against the closed door. The couch sat on the other side of the room, staring accusingly at her. It seemed to taunt her with visions and memories of the other night.

Waking up next to Ronnie had been embarrassing and lovely, all rolled into one mass of confusing feelings. Jamaica suddenly ached to be held in his arms again. But he wasn't here and based on the lack of communication, she guessed he wished to forget the entire incident.

What if what Brenda Tardash had said was true? What if he was spoken for and he had cheated on Brenda with Jamaica? Though it seemed like fitting payback, Jamaica knew two wrongs didn't make a right. If he really belonged to Brenda, then so be it. And damn him for using her.

But a part of her couldn't help feeling it was wonderful to have finally fulfilled the desires and dreams of having Ronnie just once. Of being able to say yes, instead of no. Of knowing what a caring, gentle, and passionate lover he was. Too bad his sincerity and honesty couldn't be trusted.

Hadn't she known that? Of course, she had. The whole chaotic mess they were in now was because of his lack of honesty. If he had told her when they met up at O'Toole's Tavern, what he was up to, she could have stopped him right then and there. His store never would have opened and she would not be on the brink of bankruptcy. Worse yet, she would not have to face her father in three months' time and tell him she didn't have the loan repayment of Grandpa Jones' inheritance. That somehow, he was going to have to do without the comforts of home health aides and visiting nurses.

That his only child had failed him.

The alarm on her watch began to ring. It was five minutes to closing. Sufficiently tired for the night, Jamaica walked to the front door and locked it, turned the sign around and started heading to the kitchen area. She was going home for the day. No cooking, no baking, no bookkeeping. The only thing she wanted was a glass of wine and some cheese and crackers for dinner. Maybe she'd actually watch a movie for a change. Do something, anything to not think about the situation.

Banging on the front door of the shop sent her back into the front room. Standing at the door was Ronnie. Jamaica stood on her side of the door and called through it, "What do you want, Caswell?"

Ronnie shuffled his feet, tapping his umbrella on the stoop. Only then did Jamaica notice it was pouring rain outside. "I need to talk to you for a minute."

Jamaica unlocked the door and let him in. "Make it quick, I'm tired and want to go home."

"I wanted to thank you for signing the contract, you know, for the contest. It's a pretty brave thing to do."

"Okay, fine. Enough said. Can you go now?"

"Don't you have a few minutes for me? Geez, I finally get a chance to come over and see you and you want to run off."

"Well, you haven't exactly been beating a path to my door, front or back one. I guess you got what you wanted."

"That's not it. I've been spending my free time at the police department, working with them on your robbery case. I told them my theory about Gary Standler's motive and his mistake in robbing the wrong ice cream shop. Between my own store and visits to the P.D., I don't have a lot of free time."

Jamaica plunked her hand on her hip. "Enough time for Brenda Tardash. You managed to collect her kiss this morning, didn't you?"

Ronnie's forehead furrowed as his eyebrows drew together. "What the hell are you talking about?"

"Brenda was in here to let me know that you and she are dating and that you are 'spoken for.'"

His eyes widened. "That's bullshit. She kissed me. I did not reciprocate. I told Brenda I wasn't interested way back in July. She and I are not having any kind of a relationship. I merely accepted her offer to help at my booth during the festival."

"Really? How can I trust you? How can I trust what you say and do? Truth is, I can't."

Ronnie stood, arms outstretched with palms forward, "Jamaica, for Pete's sake, give me a chance. I've been working my ass off trying to get ready for this festival, working with the police and waiting on customers at the store. How much more can I do? What can I do to make you see I'm telling the truth?"

"Probably nothing, Ronnie. I don't think there is anything you can do that could make me trust you except maybe close your store."

"I can't do that. It's my livelihood. Every cent I have is sunk into my place. If it goes under, I'm destitute. I can't live up to my high school superlative 'Least Likely to Succeed.'"

Jamaica thought about it for a minute. They were both in the same position. Each of them would lose everything if their business closed down.

"I can't lose either. I've poured my heart and soul and every penny I own into this shop. I've borrowed money to get it running and still have to pay it back. By December, in fact."

MELT MY HEART

They were silent for a few minutes both staring at the other. He looked all around the shop, as if assessing the filigree work and special ordered tables and chairs in Victorian style. *Does he realize how expensive it all was? Did he understand she was telling the truth about the amount of money she had spent renovating the Emporium and making it her own.* She hoped he did.

"Let's try to forget the stores for a little while and just be together. I enjoyed our time together the other night. I'd like to spend more time with you...get to know the adult Jamaica Jones."

She shook her head. "I don't think it's wise."

"Why not?"

"Ronnie, you can't give me what I want in a relationship. I want honesty, trust, security, and someday, I'd like a house and a family."

Ronnie flung his arms out wide. "You're right. I can give you the first three, but I can't give you the house and family. I don't have them myself and I don't know when, or if, I ever will. And I'm afraid what my past as a cop might do to my future."

"What do you mean?"

"Like Gary Standler. I don't want a family I have to look out for and worry about constantly. Worry that some idiot from my patrol days will come back and hurt any family I have. It's better to not have one than to worry about one," Ronnie said.

Jamaica stepped closer. They stood eye to eye. "Maybe you're right to worry. I knew you couldn't give me what I want. Let's shake hands, wish each other good luck and leave it at that." It wasn't what she wanted. But she couldn't risk being hurt again, and God knows, Ronnie had the capacity to hurt her.

Ronnie stared at her, eyes drawn, lips thin. Finally, he held out his hand.

They shook hands, and Ronnie left without another word.

***

"So, are you all set for the fair?" Mary asked between spoonfuls of her mint chocolate chip ice cream with hot fudge sauce sundae.

"As best I can be." Jamaica said before a bite of her own coffee ice cream, hot fudge sundae. "According to the rules, I can only serve five flavors, in either a cup, or sugar or cake cone. I think it's meant to level the field for direct comparisons."

"But that leaves all your very best ice creams and toppings out of contention." Mary exclaimed, setting down her spoon.

"I know. I agree completely." The dull ache in Jamaica's gut deepened and widened. Tears started to roll down her cheeks as she poked at her sundae with her spoon. "I know my ice cream is great. But it's a whole package. The ice cream, the sauces, the toppings, the fresh whipped cream. Stripping it down to just the ice cream – I don't know, Mary. I'm afraid."

Mary set her cup down and enfolded Jamaica in her arms. "Don't you worry, young lady. Everything will work out. Have you ever heard the phrase, 'When a door closes, a window opens.'?"

"Yeah, I've heard something like that." Jamaica sniffled, wiping her eyes with her shirt sleeve. "I just can't see how I'll survive if I have to shut my shop down."

"We're not meant to see the future, dear. We have to have faith." Mary tucked a wisp of hair back from Jamaica's face. "Pray to your momma. She'll help you get through these difficulties."

"I don't think she hears me anymore. I don't think she's listening." Jamaica's tears renewed, her heart re-tearing at the old wound.

"I'll bet she's letting you know she's around." Mary hugged her close again. "Have you been finding any coins on the ground? Or feathers?"

Jamaica pulled back to look in Mary's eyes. "Yes, but how does—"

"Spirits can't talk to us directly, so they let us know they're around by leaving coins, especially pennies. Or feathers." Mary smiled. "So, you have been finding coins?"

"All over the place. Lots of pennies, but dimes and nickels too." Jamaica dried her eyes again. "Do you really think it's my mom?"

"Of course. She's letting you know she's here for you. Talk to her and let her know you know she's here. She'd like that."

"How do you know?"

"Because I'm a mother. Mothers always like to know their children are thinking of them."

Jamaica picked up her soupy ice cream and finished it quickly. "I have to be going. I better get some sleep. Or try."

"Yes. You need some good sleep." Mary walked her to the door. "Thank you for bringing my sundae and staying to talk. And keep your chin up. What's that saying? 'It's not over until the fat lady sings.'?"

"Something like that. Good night, Mary."

"Good night, Jamaica. Sweet dreams tonight, darling."

CHAPTER NINETEEN

In the early morning of the 118th annual Fulton River Festival, forecasters predicted a hot, sunny day with intermittent clouds, temperatures in the mid-nineties. Perfect weather for ice cream. Jamaica was looking forward to making a killing at the festival *and* winning the tasting contest.

The grounds of the elementary school were serving as the festival location. The school cafeteria served as "Judgement Hall" for the competitions of cooking specialties, and artistic and original crafts. An outdoor tent held the local grange's vegetable, fruit, and flower arrangement competitions. Amusement rides had lined up in a mown meadow beside the soccer field. The merry-go-round was already spinning, the carnival music blaring across the festival grounds.

Two rows of twenty booths were lined up, facing each other with wide forty-foot aisles between them. Local merchants and organizations were filling the booths. All trying to either get the word out about their business or sell goods. Local organizations were looking for new members and fundraising, selling everything from popcorn to Girl Scout cookies. Food stand workers were prepping food for the coming crowds. The smell of hot grease wafted through the air.

The Vermont Ice Cream Emporium had booth number ten, smack dab in the middle of the first row. Fulton's Creamery and Confections' booth was across the aisle, number thirty. When she first saw the placement of the booths, Jamaica worried their lines would intermingle, perhaps tussle. But she liked the idea of always being able to see how Caswell was doing.

"Here you are, Jam. That's everything from the truck." Kevin tilted the hand truck upright, setting the stack of cardboard boxes on the ground. "Where do you want 'em?"

MELT MY HEART

"Thank you, thank you! Kevin, I don't know what I would have done if you hadn't offered to help me today." She gave him a quick hug. "Slide them over to the side there. Do us a favor and cut them open so we don't have to do it in a hurry later." Jamaica checked around the inside of the ten-foot square booth. Wooden, it was made and erected by the local fire department who used them for their annual firemen's carnival in May. One ice cream freezer sat near the front counter of the booth. Behind the booth was a freezer truck holding extra tubs of ice cream she hoped to sell throughout the day.

In front of the ice cream freezer was a small folding table holding the money box and would also hold the ballots. Vera August, one of the Merchants Association members would be handing out one ballot to each buyer, provided the customer didn't have an ink stamp on his or her left hand. Only one ballot could be cast per customer at the voting booth near the bingo stands. Once it was cast, an ink stamp would be placed on the left hand. They could still continue to taste the ice cream, but they could not vote again.

Ronnie also had a ballot distributor, Warren Howard, from Suds 'Em Up Laundromat. He also had Brenda helping him in his booth.

Good luck with her, Jamaica smirked.

Mr. Salters had told them balloting would begin at the official start of the festival, at eleven o'clock, just after the parade. The voting would close at four, though ballots would be tallied throughout the day by the head librarian, Mrs. Colleen Andrews. At five o'clock, during the closing ceremony, the winner of the tasting contest would be revealed.

At ten o'clock, the fire station horn blew, signaling the start of the parade. Mr. Salters estimated it would finish in a half an hour. Jamaica circled the tiny booth, took a sip of water, and spat it out. She didn't want to have to pee in the midst of the contest. Thanking herself for choosing to wear jeans and a tee shirt instead of her usual Victorian attire, she sat on the edge of the booth's side lost in thought.

"Jamaica." A quivering, elderly voice called out.

She glanced up as she straightened a stack of ice cream cups. "Mary!"

"You know I had to come and wish you luck." Mary grabbed at Jamaica's apron, pulling her over the edge of the booth and planted a kiss on her cheek.

"Thank you."

"Jamaica!" Her father's voice called out.

She turned to greet him. "Dad! How did you get here?"

"Senior citizens bus. I'm glad to see you too." He gave her a kiss. Sydney looked over at Mary.

"Dad, this is my friend, Mary Kettlebrook. Mary this is my dad, Sydney Jones."

He tapped his index finger on his cheek, his eyes questioning. "Do I know you?"

"Sydney?" Mary stared at him, a tentative smile of recognition breaking out on her face. "Sydney! Did you grow up in Brattleboro?"

"Mary Ferris?"

"Mary Kettlebrook now."

"You two know each other?" Jamaica looked from one to the other, her eyes widened.

"Oak Grove Elementary School." Mary said smiling more broadly than Jamaica had ever seen. Even Mary's eyes twinkled.

"Home of the Owls." Sydney added. He held out the crook of his arm. Mary slipped her hand into it. The two former classmates sidled up to each other and commenced talking like they had never stopped being classmates. Jamaica watched, forgotten as they walked off toward the picnic tables. *Well, how do you like that? Is my father Mary's long-lost school love?*

"Hey, Jam." A familiar voice called to her from the right. It was Ronnie. He approached from his booth, walking around to the side of her booth.

MELT MY HEART

"What, Caswell?" she replied, not sure which way this conversation would go but ready for anything.

He held out his hand. She noticed it trembled slightly and his face looked drawn. "Good luck to you."

Jamaica was stunned silent. She hadn't thought he'd say that. "Good luck to you, too." She shook his hand quickly and let go.

A loud, female voice called out across the alleyway. It was Brenda. "Good luck, Jamaica. You're going to need it!" She giggled until Ronnie walked over and said something to her, his face flushed and brow furrowed. Afterwards, Brenda, now with downcast eyes, looked like she was going to cry.

"Wow, I always knew she was pain, but I had no idea what a little bitch she was." Kevin stared over the counter at the sassy blonde.

The sound of the high school marching band came ever closer. With it, would be the crowd. Jamaica shivered. She prayed. She tried to remember the number she had predetermined was the break-even amount for the day. If she made $6,548.00, she could finish paying off the money she owed her father, pay her bills for another month, and get back on her feet. That was if she won the contest. Jamaica prayed again, a lot harder.

People flocked in like locusts, swarming in every direction, as soon as the parade was over. In seconds, the line outside Jamaica's booth went from none to over forty. It was hard to tell. As she had feared, her lines were merging with Ronnie's lines. It was going to be an exasperating experience for the customers. *Let's hope they don't take out their frustrations over the lines at the voting booth.*

It took a little while, but the three of them, Vera, Kevin, and Jamaica, finally got into a groove behind the counter. Kevin would take the order and the money, call it back to Jamaica. She would scoop the order, hand it forward to Vera, who would hand out the ice cream and, after a hand check, would hand out a ballot. In thirty minutes, Jamaica was drenched in sweat.

The ice cream was hard as a rock. She struggled to scoop it and started to fall behind in orders.

"Jam, let me scoop for a little while. Come up here and take orders and money." Kevin said. And so, they switched positions, and continued to switch positions every thirty minutes.

As Jamaica was collecting money, $2.50 per scoop, one woman complained it this was more expensive than Ronnie's ice cream. *I never thought to see what Ronnie was charging for his ice cream,* she thought. She took a quick leave of the ordering to have a word with Kevin.

"Ronnie's undercutting my price by twenty-five cents. Do you think I should lower my price?" Jamaica whispered.

"No, let it go. If people ask, tell them quality costs a little extra but it's worth it."

Kevin was right of course, she didn't have to match his price, though she had to wonder how many votes the difference of a quarter might be costing her.

Questions about the price difference were rare and when Jamaica gave the retort, the asking party accepted it and remained quiet.

Mr. Salters came over to the booth at one o'clock, bringing hamburgers, French fries, and sodas for all three of them. The greasy fries and burger tantalized Jamaica's nose. Other than a couple bites of the burger and a few fries, Jamaica didn't stop for lunch. Kevin managed to wolf down his meal, while Vera was replaced by another Merchants Association helper, so she could sit down and eat.

"No rest for the wicked, eh, Jam," Kevin said.

"Nope, you better not let your wife hear you say that." Jamaica smiled and hitched her head over to the right.

Kevin looked over to find his wife and kids standing in line, about ten feet away from the counter. He gave them a wave and went back to work. He'd see them soon enough.

At three o'clock, Mr. Salters came around again, suggesting they try to get as many more people through the lines as possible before

MELT MY HEART

four o'clock. The lines had been continuous the entire day, much to Jamaica's amazement. It seemed everyone from Fulton River and all the surrounding towns had come to participate in the ice cream contest. Even so, Jamaica still had a lot of ice cream left. Ice cream she didn't want to have to lug back to the shop. *How to get rid of more ice cream?*

The solution was pretty simple. A sale. An ice cream sale. Jamaica stopped Kevin, told him the new price, and then made up a new price sign: $2.25. She posted the new sign over the old sign, earning a cheer from the crowd lined up to order.

As she had hoped, the line grew a little longer at the discounted price. *Will it help sell off the extra ice cream?*

Minutes later, a cheer went up from the crowd in front of Ronnie's booth. Kevin leaned over. "Um, don't look now, but I think we have a price war going. Ronnie just lowered his ice cream to $2.00."

Jamaica looked over at Ronnie's booth and saw the crowd jostling to get closer to the front of the line. Worse, she saw some of the people in her own line, leave it to go to Ronnie's booth. Amid the chaos, Brenda was standing on something, a box perhaps, shouting to the crowd, enticing them to step up for the best ice cream in town. As Jamaica watched, Brenda flirted with several of the men in line, handing out cones and distributing kisses.

Horrified, Jamaica quickly penned a new price on a piece of cardboard and placed it over the last price sign. Applause sounded at the new price, with a few cheers.

"Kevin, we're down to $2.00 per scoop." Walking back to the freezers, she resumed scooping.

A few of the deserters returned into her line, jostling the crowd trying to retake their last position in line. Others in line elbowed them back. A dispute broke out between two large guys, one of whom had stayed in line and one who had left and then returned. Fists rose and nearly began to fly and might have if the people around hadn't separated the two men, throwing the defector to the back of the line.

Jamaica started doing the math in her head. She figured they had done over two thousand ice creams, some of them double scoops. It meant she might have already brought in over five thousand. But if she could keep at it until the end, perhaps continue selling ice cream, without ballots, after the four o'clock time, she might break even.

Her concentration was broken by the roar of the crowd across the alleyway.

"Looks like he's done it again. I think he's down to $1.75 now," Kevin said.

Flabbergasted, Jamaica stared across at Ronnie's booth. Again, people in her line moved over to his line, infiltrating those already standing in line. Much like her own experience, several skirmishes and arguments occurred.

"Don't do it, Jam. It's low enough." Kevin warned when he saw Jamaica reach for the marking pen.

"I have to Kevin. I have to get rid of this ice cream any way I can. And I need those votes." She scribbled down a new price. She posted the sign, receiving a house-raising cheer from the crowd around her booth. "It's $1.50, Kevin. Per scoop."

Feeling faint, but also giddy with terror and excitement, Jamaica went back to scooping her heart out.

In minutes, the crowd at Ronnie's booth roared again.

Kevin craned his neck to see above the crowd. He shook his head and dropped his chin to his chest.

"Oh no, now what?"

"You don't want to know," Kevin shook his head.

"Tell me!"

"One dollar."

A dollar? One dollar? That was insane.

She grabbed the marking pen and another piece of cardboard and wrote. She hung the sign and returned to her post. The crowd went wild. People cheered, roared, jumped, and pushed toward the front counter.

"Why not give it away for free?" someone called.

"The rules of the contest say I can't." Jamaica yelled back in the direction of the questioner. "One cent, folks. Get your pennies ready."

Everyone at Ronnie's booth left it, pushing into the crowd around Jamaica's booth.

Jamaica scooped until Mr. Salters came around to end the contest, collecting the last of the ballots. Then she pulled down the price signs and put up one saying, "CLOSED."

Exhausted, Jamaica scanned the remaining people in the alleyway. The crowds had thinned. Parents with small children had left to feed their broods something more nutritious than festival fare at home.

Her eye caught on one silhouette standing on the far side of the Girl Scout booth, one booth away from Ronnie's. The hair on the back of her neck bristled. The man, of medium height and wild, sandy brown hair stood intently watching the crowds milling in front of Ronnie's booth. His gray sweatshirt was baggy over his dirty jeans which hung low over sneakers that had seen many years of use. As realization descended, she scurried out of her booth, sprinting toward Ronnie's; cutting, and shoving to get to the front of the line.

"Ronnie!" she yelled out. "Ronnie!"

Ronnie looked up as he was handing over a cone of chocolate ice cream. He watched as she got closer. He must have read something in the look on her face.

"Ronnie! The robber! I just saw him. He's here." Jamaica yelled when she reached him at the front of the line.

"What? He's here? Now?" Ronnie's face lit up, his eyes wide, suddenly scanning the crowd before him.

"Next booth over. On the far side," she reported, pointing in the direction.

"Brenda, take over for me!" he ordered and scooted around the rear of his booth, exiting to meet up with Jamaica.

Ronnie sprinted past her heading for his car. "What's he wearing?" he yelled over his shoulder.

"Gray sweatshirt, dirty blue jeans, and sneakers."

"Any sign of a gun?" Ronnie asked as he reached into his car's glove compartment, pulling out a shiny blue gun. Next, he pulled out a pair of handcuffs.

"I didn't notice one," Jamaica said, suddenly more afraid. Her hands shook and her knees weakened.

Ronnie shoved the gun in the waistband of his jeans, the handcuffs in his pocket, and turned toward her. "I don't want you getting hurt." Leaning over, he kissed her forehead.

"You can't go after him with a gun in this crowd!" Jamaica exclaimed. "You'll hurt someone."

"I know. I'm hoping I don't have to use it, but in case he's armed, I'd rather be prepared. He's not getting another shot at me again." Ronnie headed behind the Girl Scout booth.

Jamaica watched him go, then couldn't prevent her feet from following. Ronnie disappeared around the corner of the far side of the scouts' booth. She quickly bolted over to look around the corner.

From her vantage point she could see Ronnie, bent over, staying low behind a small crowd of teenagers. Gary Standler still stood exactly where she had spotted him before, leaning against the far corner of the booth, watching the crowd in front of the booths.

If he'd been watching Ronnie, he must not have seen him leave his booth. Ronnie's movements roused the suspicions of the teenagers. He held a finger to his closed mouth to prevent them from saying anything but one floppy haired boy called out, "Hey man, what ya doing?"

The words caught the attention of Gary Standler, who turned around, spotted Ronnie and bolted across the fairgrounds. Weaving through the crowd, Standler headed for the nearest wood line, behind the football field to the left. Ronnie sprinted after him, trying to follow him through the crowd.

As she watched in horror, Ronnie tried to tackle him from behind. The two men fell to the ground in a heap. They tussled a moment before Standler scrambled to his feet and ran. Ronnie lay where he dropped, his hands grasping his thigh, his face wracked with pain.

Jamaica turned on her heels and ran behind the booths, dodging the cars and carts of supplies, boxes, and product paraphernalia. She reached the end of the line of booths just in time to see Gary Standler about to break free of the crowd and start heading across the football field. She swung over to the right, running as hard and fast as she could and hit Standler broadside as he emerged from the crowd.

They both went down, hitting the ground so hard Jamaica was sure she heard his teeth crack. By the time Jamaica came up on all fours, she saw Ronnie, with his gun trained down on Standler, telling him to freeze. The man stopped moving, his arms and legs splayed out on the ground. Ronnie wrenched his arms behind his back and applied the handcuffs.

"Jamaica, frisk him good, honey. All over," Ronnie ordered.

She got up and gave him such a thorough pat down they probably should have been married. At the small of Standler's back, Jamaica found a gun. She pulled it out gingerly between her thumb and index finger, unsure if it was loaded or if the safety was on.

As she handed the gun to Ronnie, the Fulton River police arrived.

They secured the scene, walked Standler to their cruiser and stuffed him in the back of the vehicle before taking brief statements from both Jamaica and Ronnie.

They both watched as the cruiser drove away.

Ronnie turned on her, his eyes flashing. "I thought I told you to stay put."

"You never said any such thing, not that I'd have listened to you anyway," Jamaica snapped, pushing hair out of her face. "It's a good thing I didn't or you'd still be chasing him across the field and through the woods."

They were both silent for a few seconds.

He looked down as he rubbed his thigh. "I guess I owe you a thank you. Though it was pretty stupid to tackle him if you weren't sure if he had a gun."

"I didn't even think about a gun."

Ronnie rolled his eyes to heaven. "I, eh, better go see how the booth is doing."

"Don't you mean, Brenda?" Jamaica couldn't help herself from giving a stinging remark.

"Yeah, I guess I do," Ronnie sighed. "She has been a big help to me today. I owe her a thank you for offering to help."

"I'm sure she's looking for more than a thank you," Jamaica taunted.

"A thank you is all she's getting."

Silence.

"Well. I'll see you at the voting booth in a little while." Ronnie said.

"Yeah. See you there." Jamaica watched Ronnie head back to his booth.

Exhausted, starving, thirsty, and stressed out, she walked back to her booth. The smell of the greasy foods turned her stomach as she passed the food stands. Wearily, she climbed into the cab of her rented freezer truck. The irritating music from the carousel droned through the closed door into her aching brain. Laying her head down on the steering wheel she sobbed until she didn't have any more tears to shed. It had all been too much for one day. The contest, the price war, the apprehension of Gary Standler. And another argument with Ronnie.

A knock on the door of the truck brought her back to reality. It was Kevin. He had the money box. It was stuffed full of bills and coins. He handled her a bottle of water and she chugged the entire bottle.

"Can you take the money box some place safe, maybe to your own store for the night? I don't want to deal with it tonight."

"Sure, no problem. Um, Jam, it's almost five o'clock. They're going to announce the winner in about five minutes. Don't you want to go over to the voting booth to hear the results?"

"I'm not sure I want to hear the results, Kev."

"Course you do. You've got this. You're Jamaica Jones. The best ice cream maker in Fulton River. I'll bet you a thousand dollars, you're the winner." The fierceness in his voice buoyed her spirits for a moment.

"I haven't got a spare thousand to bet with." Jamaica painfully got out of the truck, realizing how much her body ached after tackling Standler. She'd go hear what the results were. Then she'd pack everything up. Trying to make her goal might be a lost cause.

The walk over to the voting booth took forever. Light-headedness and exhaustion made Jamaica's way slow. A large crowd had gathered around it impeding her progress. As she approached, she heard her name being called over the PA. "Jamaica Jones, please come to the voting booth."

When people realized she was trying to get through, they stepped aside for her. She hated this. She would hate to have to keep a stiff upper lip if the results were bad. Her insides quivered, her stomach rolled, and her vision spun.

"I'm here," her voice wavered as she got to the front of the voting booth. Gingerly, she climbed the steps up on to the stage.

Mr. Salters waved her over. "Ah, there you are. We wanted to announce the winner of the tasting contest, but both contestants weren't present."

Ronnie sidled up to her, standing by her side as Colleen Andrews, took the microphone.

"I am pleased to announce the winner of the Fulton River Festival Ice Cream Contest," she said. "It was a tight race. The winner has won by a margin of only thirty-five ballots."

"Who is it?" someone in the rear of the crowd yelled.

"Patience, young man."

"The winner of the first Fulton River Festival Ice Cream Contest is Fulton's Creamery and Confections."

Jamaica heard the words and the bottom fell out of her world.

CHAPTER TWENTY

"You're late again." Sydney opened the door for his daughter.

"Good morning, Daddy. Good to see you too!" Jamaica breezed past him into the kitchen and began getting his breakfast ready. "Nice of you to cut me some slack after yesterday."

He stopped her by the elbow and wrapped his frail arms around her. She rested her chin on his shoulder. "I'm sorry you didn't win, sweetheart. You should have."

"Yeah, well. Shit happens. I made a bet and I lost." She gave him a squeeze before shimmying out of his arms. "How about eggs, breakfast sausage, and toast today?" She urged while pouring herself a cup of coffee.

"Nope. Oatmeal." He sat down at the table and picked up yesterday's newspaper, reading the sports page or at least looking at the pictures. Jamaica couldn't tell which.

She ground her back molars, put back the eggs and pulled out the cardboard canister of old-fashioned rolled oats. "So, I didn't realize you knew Mary Kettlebrook."

He dropped the paper to look at her. "I didn't either. I knew her as Mary Ferris. Ferris was her maiden name. Kettlebrook is her married name."

"Ah, I see." Jamaica plated his breakfast and set it before him. "So how was it, catching up with her?"

"Great! We have a date tomorrow night at bingo."

She watched as her father dug into his oatmeal. "A date? Wow, I didn't realize it was so serious."

"At our age, we don't have time to waste."

"I guess not." Jamaica said, before proceeding to boil up a couple of eggs as she usually did. Then she picked up his apartment.

Her father grabbed her arm as she walked by on the way to the sink. "You're not bent out of shape about that, are you? Me and Mary seeing each other?"

Truth was Jamaica's brain and heart were a whirlpool of emotions. On the one hand, she was happy to know the two old friends had found each other again. Her father didn't socialize with other people generally, and Mary didn't either. Yet, she couldn't help but feel her mother's memory was somehow being trampled with the renewed friendship and possible relationship. And this was not something she could talk to her father about, ever.

"Don't look like that. Mary and I go back a long way. It's been more than sixty years since she and I met on the playground in grammar school. We were sweet on each other long before I met your mother." Sydney took his daughter's hand and held it firmly. "But I loved your mother. Don't ever doubt that. And nothing and no one is going to change that either."

"Yes. I know." Tears welled up in her eyes and she wiped them away with her fingers.

"She's gone, Jamaica. Ten years now. I didn't forget. I think of her and how much I miss her every single day. That's not going to change. Not even with Mary around." He wrapped his arms around Jamaica. They clung together, something Jamaica realized they hadn't done in a long time. It felt good, comforting.

"No Dad, I'm happy for you both." She smiled and found a good part of her truly meant it. Her world may be falling apart, but she could be happy and grateful her father was looking brighter.

"Good, now, get out of here. I'm sure you have things to do at the shop. I'll take care of the dishes."

Jamaica gave him a hard stare. Her father offering to do the dishes? The earth had really shifted off its axis if he was willing to do housework. "Okay, thanks, Daddy." She kissed his forehead and left, all the while marveling at the transformation brought about by love.

MELT MY HEART

***

Jamaica huffed and threw the Fulton River Gazette on the kitchen work table. Her jaw clenched and her muscles tense, she stomped to the back door and looked out into the parking lot. *How dare he take all the credit for catching Standler!*

She walked to the far side of the room and kicked the couch. Walking back to the table, she picked up the newspaper and re-read the article.

> "There was lots of excitement at this year's Fulton River Festival. Top among the events was the ice cream war between Vermont Ice Cream Emporium and Fulton's Creamery and Confections. Both owners entered the contest seeking the "Best Ice Cream in Fulton River" prize. Mr. Ronald Caswell won the title, giving his shop the right to continue operation in Fulton River. The losing shop owner, Ms. Jamaica Jones must close up shop as part of the agreed upon arrangement. Also during the festival, Ronald Caswell, caught a criminal on the loose. A retired police officer, Mr. Caswell pursued Gary Standler through the festival crowd finally tackling him. The apprehended man was found to have a stolen pistol on his person."

I found the pistol! Jeeze, where did this reporter get his information from? Would Ronnie throw me under the bus like this?

> "Standler was inadvertently released from prison months ago when he was mistaken for a different individual with the same last name. Fulton River Police Chief Kirk Werner said 'Mr. Caswell deserves a medal for his bravery in the face of grave danger. This town is indebted to his heroism.' Mayor Marguerite D'Anguerra concurs. Her staff is working on a formal presentation in the coming months."

"A medal? Seriously?" Jamaica sputtered, rolling her eyes to heaven, and shaking her head. She crushed the newspaper with a growl and threw it in the trash can.

***

The days after the festival went by in a blur for Ronnie. Local, state, and national news outlets heard of the event and descended on Fulton's

Creamery and Confections. Now famous, the store was mobbed with well-wishers from the area and a plethora of curious tourists, from as far away as New York City, Boston, and even Quebec City.

With the increased business, Ronnie had to hire a small work crew. He managed to find some older, retired folks looking for part-time work. People he could trust to follow instructions. So far, they had worked out well, serving customers while Ronnie did news interviews, TV spots, and tried to keep up with the ordering and supply needs of the shop.

Within a week, it was obvious to him, he needed an assistant manager. One afternoon, the day after the advertisement for an assistant manager was printed in the local newspaper, the doorbell jingled. Knowing his hired help would serve the customer, Ronnie ignored it and resumed making his candy order. Then he heard the clickity-clack of kitten heels on the floor tile. *That can only be one person*, he thought with an audible groan.

Brenda Tardash's head popped around the entry way. "Ronnie, I'm so glad to see you. I have something for you." She placed a piece of paper on the desk in front of him.

Ronnie picked up the paper and scanned the list. "What's this?" He frowned, trying to make sense of the list.

"Why, it's my resume, silly. I'm here to apply for the assistant manager's job, of course." Brenda beamed a smile of spectacular wattage at him. "We worked so well together at the fair. It makes perfect sense to continue. We're the dynamic duo. You know, like Batman and Robin."

Frowning deeper, Ronnie dropped the paper on his desk. There was no way on earth he'd hire Brenda, but he'd humor her for now. He leaned over to his left and extracted a sheet of paper from the drawer. "Here, fill this out," he said, a little more curtly than he wanted to sound.

Brenda recoiled from the paper. "I don't need to fill that out, Ronnie. You know everything you need already. We were a great team at the festival. We're going to make a great team here, sweetheart."

Ronnie dropped the paper on his desk. "Don't call me sweetheart. I'm not your sweetheart."

Sashaying a little closer to him, Brenda lifted her hand to touch Ronnie's arm, but he was quicker. Jumping back in his chair, he abruptly stood and withdrew out of reach, leaving the chair between them.

"Don't be like that Ronnie. You know we're perfect for each other. We have been since high school."

He held up his palms at chest level. "I'm not going to say it again, so listen carefully, Brenda. We never had anything in high school. And we're not starting up now." Steepling his hands, he motioned them with every word for emphasis. "I'm not interested in starting anything up. Not with you."

Her mouth dropped open and she stepped back with her hand over her heart as though mortally wounded. "Ronnie, darling, please don't be that way!"

Scrubbing a hand over his reddening face, Ronnie replied, "There's no other way to be. Now, please leave my store and don't come back."

"But, what about my application?" Brenda cried as tears stormed down her checks.

"No, Brenda. Thank you for the offer but under the circumstances, I think it's best if I decline your offer."

"But Ronnie –," she cried.

"Leave," Ronnie shouted, pointing to the door, all the fury he had been holding in erupting.

Brenda turned and ran for the door. She was out in a flash and gone. Ronnie became aware of the people in the store staring at him with eyes wide and mouths agape.

His face flushed hot as he tried to make a quiet withdrawal into his office. After closing the curtain, Ronnie sat down at his desk. He picked up Brenda's resume, crumpled it up and tossed it into the trash can. Next, he pulled open the lower right desk drawer. The bottle of Scotch was almost empty. *Have to get a new bottle tomorrow.* He downed the last of the fiery liquid straight from the bottle, as he chastised himself for agreeing to let Brenda help at the festival.

***

Jamaica hid. Every time someone saw her, they asked what she would do next. The truth was she had not a clue. Several times she had read and re-read the contest contract and damned herself for insisting the losing owner should stop business immediately. She couldn't sell it as an ice cream shop. She didn't want to sell anything. Not one chair and table set. Not until she figured out her next move. So, packing up the salvageable goods, and the non-perishable items, and her kitchen supplies became her immediate chore.

She hadn't told anyone about her trips to all the banks in town. Nor, her long talk on the phone with the credit union. She had to give them credit for their patience as they all listened to her dilemma. Many of them had sent her off with a worksheet to fill out, listing her assets (not many beyond the contents of the store) and liabilities (also not many). Having refurbished the shop using her own personal money, she had never set up lines of credit with any financial institutions. It, she was told, was an "unfortunate mistake."

If she had lines of credit, at least she would have a business credit history. Her own credit history, while good and admirable, wasn't applicable. Even her good history paying the landlord and utilities didn't help much. Neither did the nearly six thousand dollars she made at the festival. In fact, it didn't help at all.

She had gone as far as Montpelier for more options, including the Small Business Administration. There had been no help there. Not a single bank in Vermont would lend her enough money to change her business. Jamaica was stuck.

One thing she was only temporarily stuck with was her stock of ice cream. She still had seventeen five-gallon tubs of it, in twelve different flavors left in her freezers, along with an assortment of sorbets and ice cream confections such as sandwiches, pies, and cakes.

The contract said she couldn't sell ice cream after she lost. Instead, Jamaica had made arrangements to donate the items to various town organizations as either fundraising materials or volunteer appreciation parties. If it all had to go, it was best for it to be used for good purposes. Either way, it would help as a tax write-off at the end of the year.

Now, she often found herself, teary-eyed, wandering the shop with nothing to do, except watch the line of customers waiting to get inside Ronnie's store. Her heart ached over the loss of her shop. She could only describe it to her father as if she had lost a child, because her shop, her baby, was as precious to her. It was something she had built from scratch, refurbished, nurtured, and raised from its early infancy into the sophisticated ice cream parlor it was today. No place else in Vermont served the types and varieties of products she did. Or had. And it killed her to see it was over.

She wondered why destiny had brought her to this low level. What was she now that she could no longer be the proprietress of the Emporium? Who was she now? The thoughts swirled in her head in her every waking moment. What was to become of her?

And what was she going to do about Burpy? How could she care for him without a steady income? Who would feed him if she didn't? Would the next tenant of this shop space welcome him at the back door and take care of him like she did? The security deposit on the shop would only keep her in the building another two months unless she could come up with a new plan and more money. Questions filled her brain all the while she contemplated her future. *Is there anything that isn't going wrong?*

The only thing she could say that was going right was her father. Sydney Jones was recuperating from his fractured arm. In a couple more weeks, the doctors would remove his plaster cast. It would mean the end of the visiting nurses and the home health aides as well. The insurance and Medicare would stop covering the expenses. He would be back to covering the cost with his own money.

Jamaica knew the fractured arm was not a good thing to have happened, but it had come at a serendipitous time, when her father had needed financial help covering his medical assistance bills. She thanked God for the divine intervention but knew her time was up. Regardless of the fact it wasn't yet December, she was going to have to repay the loan money now when her father desperately needed it.

"Hey Daddy," Jamaica called out as she entered her father's senior-living apartment. She spied the top of his head peeping over the top cushion of his recliner.

"Is that you, Jamaica?" he called out over the blaring sound of the television.

"Yes, it's me. Who else would have a key to your apartment?" she quipped as she planted a kiss on his forehead.

"No one I know of, though the super has a key to every apartment in case of emergency."

"Good thing." She took a seat on the sofa, perpendicular to his chair. "I've brought you something." She reached into her purse, pulling out the business check.

"What's that, Pumpkin?" he asked, reaching on the side table for his reading glasses with one hand as he took the check with the other. Putting on the glasses, he looked at the slip of paper in his hand.

Jamaica saw his eyes tear up. "Ah, Daddy, don't cry."

"I can't help it. You have no idea how much it means to me to have you repay this now."

"I know. I know you're needing it and it's time I paid up."

Sydney took off his glasses and wiped away his tears. "Are you sure you can do this? I know you're in a real jam since you lost the contest. Are you sure you can afford to repay me?"

"I am one hundred percent positive." Jamaica smiled. "Now let me make us a cup of tea," she bounded up from the sofa before her father could see her own eyes get misty. In light of her financial difficulties, repaying the loan was shooting herself in the foot. But her father deserved his money back, on time. And she would be damned if she wasn't going to provide it.

CHAPTER TWENTY-ONE

Trouble was brewing in the Caribbean and it was heading north. This year's hurricane predictions had been spot-on, with twelve tropical storms so far, four of them turning into hurricanes affecting the U.S.

On Monday, the twelfth of September, weather stations reported on tropical storm "Mindy" having glanced off the coast of Venezuela and curved toward the Windward Islands. St. Vincent, St. Lucia, Barbados, and Martinique all took direct hits from the Category Three hurricane before it pushed on to the Virgin Islands and Puerto Rico, and curved northwest to head for a landing in South Carolina. But the jet stream was low, and deeply troughed through the south, keeping the now Category Two hurricane farther out to sea, where it drew strength again from the jet stream's warmth. By Wednesday, the weathermen were all predicting a direct hit to the southern New England states of Connecticut and Rhode Island, as well as impacting Long Island, and southeastern New York, including New York City.

The people of Vermont cast a wary eye toward the news reports. They remembered the devastation suffered by Wilmington, Vermont from Hurricane Irene, which took out bridges, wiped out homes, destroying some businesses entirely, even with sufficient warning from the authorities. Many lessons were learned during that incident. Everyone kept a watchful eye on the weather reports, not just in the winter months. Even the birds kept a wary eye to the skies overhead – choosing to fly low instead of up high and wildly feeding at bird feeders all across Vermont.

People who had been through Hurricanes Sandy and Irene scurried to secure their properties and evacuate their homes, fleeing to the shelters set up by local municipalities. Old timers remembered the 1938 storm and the 1976 hurricane that also devastated the area with high winds and flooding. They especially were not going to take any chances.

MELT MY HEART

Ronnie didn't have much time to listen to the weather reports. He knew about the possible threat, but had larger, more immediate concerns to deal with than a potential hurricane. Empire Kitchens, the maker of his ice cream was shut down. A routine swab test had detected listeria, a foodborne bacterium, in their processing equipment. They had notified the health department, checked samples of previously released ice creams, and shut down production to sterilize all their equipment and identify the source of the contamination. The checked samples had not shown any contamination, though the health department had forced them to recall the last batch of ice cream made, sold to a restaurant in upstate New York.

While the recall didn't affect Ronnie, he was nervous. Listeria infections could be fatal in the elderly, newborns, persons with weakened immune systems, and it could cause stillbirths and miscarriages in pregnant women. While Empire Kitchens and the health department assured him his ice cream was fine, he couldn't help but worry. The shut down in production was a good thing in his opinion. But until Empire was back making ice cream, he would have to hold all his ice cream orders and hope he didn't run out of any flavors, especially the most popular ones.

He tried to look on the brighter side of the situation. If he did run out of some flavors, it would force people to select other, less popular flavors, perhaps finishing those tubs that might have been around a little longer. Looking in the walk-in freezer again, he reconciled the inventory list to the stock on hand. It was accurate.

The doorbell tinkled. "Hey, Jamaica?" Kevin called from the front door.

"Yes, Kev. I'm in the kitchen."

Within seconds, Kevin appeared in the doorway. "Jam, you been hearing about the hurricane heading our way?" A shocked expression filled his face. "I can't get used to seeing you in jeans and tee shirts instead of your Victorian costume."

"This is more practical now," she said, motioning toward her attire. Kevin joined Jamaica in the kitchen. "And yes, I heard about Mindy. She's supposed to make landfall on the coast of Connecticut tomorrow morning, right?"

"Yeah, I wanted to make sure you knew about it. Her track is exactly like Hurricane Irene, it hit this area pretty damn hard. You should probably start planning for a hit, just in case. The fire department is warning people close to the river that they might end up underwater."

Jamaica went pale. "There's not much I can do. Tape up the windows, I guess."

"Taping's not a good idea. Better to board up the windows."

"Can't afford to do that, I'm sure. Besides, the first floor and sidewalk are elevated off the street level. That should help if it floods."

It's not very high. If we get more than two feet, we'll have water inside our stores. I'm going to move some merchandise to higher ground. I'll stop over and give you a hand if you want to do the same." Kevin offered.

"Thanks, Kevin. I don't suppose you have a generator?"

"Sorry. And forget about finding one at the hardware store now. I stopped there this morning. They're all sold out."

"I won't have time to get one or know what to look for, anyway."

"I hear ya," he said. "Hey, got to go check on my wife's studio. I'll see you in the morning." Kevin headed out the archway to the front door.

"Bye," Jamaica called after him.

Truth was, she hadn't given it much thought, she was so wrapped up in the business problem. But if the hurricane struck, and the electricity went out, she would be really screwed. The remaining ice cream would self-insulate for a few hours but even the best freezers would lose their cool. And hers were secondhand. She could lose her entire remaining ice cream stock and have nothing to give the organizations.

To help maintain the freezer temperature as long as possible, Jamaica began consolidating the ice cream tubs into the walk-in freezer. Then she placed the frozen pies, cakes, and confections on top of the tubs. If everything were in one basket, maybe they would stay cold longer. At least she hoped it would work that way should the power go out. Next, she cleared the tables of napkin dispensers, moved the tables to the rear of the room far away from the front windows and door, and stacked the chairs on top of the tables.

With that task completed, Jamaica turned her thoughts to her father and Mary. Both were alone. She'd have to get them to a shelter if one were available, so she could stay at the shop.

Jamaica picked up her cellphone and dialed. "Hey, Daddy. How you doing?"

Sydney Jones sounded good for a change. "Hello Pumpkin, I'm good. How are you doing? You hear about the storm on the way?"

"Yeah, that's why I'm calling. I'd like to get you to a shelter. I don't want you stuck out there in the country all by yourself in case the power goes out or something happens, and you can't get out."

"I know, I talked with the neighbors. They're all going to the senior center. They said they'd take me with them. Mary's going to meet me there. Is that okay with you?" Sydney asked.

"Of course, of course. It's a perfect place for you both. They probably have a generator. Plus, they'll be able to feed you there and everything." She felt relieved someone else had also thought of her father's welfare. High on a hill top, the senior center would definitely not have to deal with flooding.

"What about you? What are you doing?" Sydney asked, a note of concern in his voice.

"I'll be at the shop, Dad. Just in case the power goes out. Don't worry, Kevin from the shop next door will be close by," Jamaica lied a little. She wasn't sure Kevin would be around during the storm. Chances were, he'd be home with his family.

"Good. You stay put once all hell breaks loose. Don't you go meandering outside once it starts. Especially if the river crests its banks."

"Don't worry, I'll stay safe."

A steady rain started by five in the morning. Jamaica awoke on the couch to the sound of its pounding on the windows.

At six, Kevin came over as promised but there was nothing for him to do. As they talked, the skies overhead darkened further, and the rain poured even more. Kevin said his goodbyes and wished Jam well as he left to join his family at home.

Alone, Jamaica wandered the floor of the shop looking for anything else she could do. Seeing nothing, she retreated to the kitchen area. For once, Jamaica wished she had a television in her shop so she could keep track of the storm information. The radio was turned on, tuned to the Brattleboro station instead of Vermont Public Radio as usual.

The weather reports were still predicting a direct hit for southern Connecticut and Rhode Island, centered on the mouth of the Connecticut River. Estimated time of landfall was presumed to be nine o'clock in the morning. About now. New predictions indicated Hurricane Mindy, Category Four at landfall, would march up the Connecticut River Valley. How far up she would ride before fizzling out was not known. Public officials and news media were all advising everyone from the coast of Long Island Sound to the Canadian border to brace for the worse. The Vermont governor had declared a state of emergency in advance of any destruction.

Her anxious pacing led her past Burpy's blanket. Where was he? Fearful she might have missed hearing him at the back door, she opened it and peered out. Without a canopy or awning, she was thoroughly soaked by the rainfall. Looking in the parking lot, there wasn't any sign of the dog. She turned to go back into the kitchen, wanting to leave the door open in case he came, but the wind was blowing the rain in all directions. It would easily pass through the screen door, soaking the kitchen floor. Reluctantly, Jamaica shut the back door and prayed she would hear the dog's scratching if he came to her.

She grabbed a dish towel to pat the rainwater from her hair. As she did, she walked into the shop's front room. Standing before the giant pane of glass, she looked out onto Main Street. Torrents of rain fell so thick Jamaica could not see beyond the buildings across the street, nor farther than a few hundred yards up and down the street. Water cascaded down the sidewalks and streets as though someone had opened a fire hydrant close by. With it came the litter: paper cups, soda cans, shreds of napkins, all probably from blown-over trash cans along Main Street.

Wringing her hands in the towel, her weight shifting from one foot to the other, Jamaica gazed out at the tempest. She turned away from the front window and returned to the kitchen.

After hanging the towel on her office chair to dry, she poured herself a cup of cold coffee. It tasted bitter from having sat too long but Jamaica knew it might be the last cup she would get for a long while.

With nothing else to do, she returned to the front window.

She gasped and set her coffee cup down on the window sill. In the short time she had been gone, the water in the street had gone from a cascade to a foot-deep raging stream. Now, not only litter but the trash bins themselves were floating by in the current.

Transfixed by the spectacle, she viewed the scene, her coffee forgotten. In minutes, she was aware the depth had increased even more, to nearly two feet now. The water now threatened to reach over the raised sidewalk of her building.

Jamaica went to the front door of the building and tried to judge the height distance between the sidewalk and her shop's threshold. It was a mere four inches.

Hands fluttering, Jamaica ran to the kitchen, her eyes searching for something – anything that could act like a sand bag to keep the water out. She spied the thirty-pound bags of flour on the supply shelves. Would they work? There was no choice but to try them. She hoisted a bag over her left shoulder and trudged to the front door. She swung the bag down off her sagging shoulder and placed it in front of the door.

She caught a glimpse of dark brown outside her door. She looked out the window. There, beyond the sidewalk, in the street was Burpy, trying to swim his way in the torrent of water.

Crying out, Jamaica pulled back the bag of flour and opened the front door. She stepped out onto the sidewalk, the water rising to her knees.

Seeing her, the dog veered toward her, but the current kept pushing him back. Despite all the paddling, the poor creature couldn't gain any ground. His black nose fought to stay above the water.

Jamaica stepped out into the street into thigh deep water. The force of the current surprised her as it pushed against her, trying to sweep her down Main Street. Her feet held steady as she reached out for Burpy. She lunged for the dog as he struggled, catching him around the neck. But as her center of gravity shifted, the current overwhelmed her compromised balance, lifting her off her feet. Together, Jamaica and the dog rode the rush of water as it swept them down the street.

Jamaica tried not to panic. She held onto the dog tightly, keeping his head above water. Stretching her feet down trying to get a toehold, she could feel the asphalt, but the strong current kept pushing her off balance. Objects struck her legs, knocking them loose as she fought for purchase on the ground. The weight of the water pressing against her chest, her breath heaved in ragged gulps.

Looking ahead for something to grab onto, Jamaica saw the Fulton River had also run over its banks. And she was headed straight for it. Hot fear spread through her body despite the cold water. If she was swept into the river, she knew it would be all over. It would be a quick trip over the falls and a short trip into the churning Connecticut River.

"JAMAICA!"

She heard a voice call out to her. Looking up in the direction it was coming from, she saw Ronnie, on the sidewalk of his own shop waving frantically at her.

"Jamaica! Over here!" he called out.

Choking on the water, she called back with a tremor in her voice, "I can't get there! Help me!"

Holding on to the dog, Jamaica tried even harder to maneuver over to the side of the street where Ronnie stood. But he was gone.

His head and shoulders bobbed through the water, using the current to his advantage, as he swam out to her in strong strokes. He grabbed her around the neck in a lifeguard's hold.

"Drop the dog!"

"No!" Jamaica cried when Ronnie flipped her onto her back, her arms clutching Burpy to her chest.

Gnashing his teeth, Ronnie checked his position and began to swim back to the sidewalk in powerful strokes, hauling Jamaica and the dog with him. In minutes they were beside the sidewalk. Ronnie swore as he stumbled onto the sidewalk. He turned around and grabbed Jamaica under the armpits, tossing her onto the elevated sidewalk to safety, the dog still clutched to her chest.

They sat there for a few seconds catching their breath.

"It's going to get deeper." Ronnie opened the door of his shop. "Let's get inside."

CHAPTER TWENTY-TWO

Jamaica tried to get on her feet but couldn't without Ronnie's help. He bent over and again, hauled her up by her armpits. All together, they entered Ronnie's shop, traipsing water as they went. They collapsed in the nearest chairs. Only then did Jamaica set Burpy down on his own four paws. Burpy shook off the water and continued to shake from the cold as did Jamaica and Ronnie. The dog plodded to a corner and laid down, a dazed expression in his eyes.

"What the hell were you doing?" Ronnie demanded as he wrung water from his wet shirt.

"I was saving the dog." Jamaica gathered her wet hair, wringing water from it.

Ronnie glared at her, shaking his head. "It was a damned fool thing to do. You could have drowned. You can't swim, remember?" he barked angrily.

"Well, I didn't. Thanks to you."

They sat a few moments, each of them trying to control their anger and calm down.

"I'm sorry." Jamaica stared at her wet sneakers, afraid of the look on his face, and sorry she had nearly killed herself, the dog, and him all in one shot.

Ronnie reached over and took her hand. He looked like he didn't know what to say at first. "I'm glad you're okay."

Ronnie got up and started walking into the back room. He turned slightly and waved her to follow. Jamaica followed slowly, giving a glance over her shoulder out the window before disappearing behind the curtain into the office area.

Bent over at the waist, he rummaged through a miniature refrigerator. He withdrew a block of cheese, a bag of sliced pepperoni, and an apple. "I don't have much, but we can share a lunch. I'll bet you didn't have lunch yet, am I right?"

"No, I mean yes. I didn't get anything for lunch yet. Wish I had known. I have a loaf of fresh bread back at the shop."

"Damn! It would have been great. But I guess we'll have to do with crackers." Ronnie smiled as he opened the lower left desk drawer and pulled out a box of saltines. Next, he opened the lower right drawer and pulled out a bottle of Scotch.

Jamaica's jaw dropped. "Wow. I guess you're prepared for anything, aren't you?"

"Hey, I never know when I'll get free for lunch. So, I keep something on hand in case I can't get over to Tony's." He blushed and would not meet her eyes. "How's it been going?"

"Still working on it. I have a couple ideas. Some require more capital investment, which makes them harder. I hope to choose soon," Jamaica fibbed. There wasn't any reason to tell Ronnie about her money issues. She would work them out somehow.

Hungry from their ordeal, they started munching on the snacks. Ronnie cut the apple in half and sliced out the core. Wiping his hands on a paper towel, he got up to get cups for the Scotch. "You like Scotch?"

"Never tried it. I'm not into hard liquor." Jamaica admitted, watching him pour a finger width of Scotch into each of the cups.

"Well, take it easy on this. Just sip," he said as he raised his cup toward her. "To new beginnings. Cheers."

Jamaica raised her cup toward him, "Cheers."

They each sipped. Jamaica broke out coughing.

"Careful. It's strong." Ronnie warned, a little too late. He grinned as she choked on the fiery liquid.

Jamaica squelched another fit of coughing and with a raspy voice said, "Yeah, figured it out fast."

Ronnie jumped up from his chair and started digging through a duffle bag beside the desk. "I almost forgot. I have a change of clothes."

He pulled out a pair of jeans and an Oxford shirt. "This is all I have. You can have it"

Jamaica blinked. She was soaked to her underwear. Her eyes brightened. "I have an idea. You take the pants and I'll take the shirt."

"What?" Ronnie's eyebrows shot up.

Jamaica took the shirt out of his hand and went into the bathroom. She returned two minutes later wearing only the dry shirt and her rain-soaked panties and bra. She nodded at the pants still hanging from his left hand. "You get the pants."

Ronnie emerged from the bathroom minutes later, the jeans tight to his body, accentuating his thighs and butt. His torso was bare, exposing his broad chest and muscular arms.

With his rumpled wet hair and tight jeans and bare chest, she couldn't help but think he looked gorgeous... Memories of his naked body on the couch in her shop came flooding back to her, bringing her lower parts to attention. Despite being her first time, she thought it had been wonderful. He was gentle, such a good lover. Not that she had anyone to compare him too. He was considerate and kind and oh, so, sexy. Given the chance, she knew she'd do it again.

But there wasn't going to be another chance. They had decided it wasn't going to work. They wanted different things out of life. They had different plans. Better to not get involved than to start something they couldn't finish. *But gosh, what a body. What a shame to waste such a ripe opportunity.*

She watched him hang their wet clothes over the ends of mop and broom handles. They dripped on the floor but he didn't seem to care. He returned to the desk, picked up his cup and downed the contents in one gulp. He hissed and made a face as the fiery liquid must have burned all the way down his esophagus.

"Yikes, what was that for?" Jamaica asked.

"I'm hoping it will warm me up quickly. The water was damn cold." He poured himself another inch of Scotch. "More?" he asked her.

"Sure." she regretted it as soon as she said it. She wasn't much of a drinker and it was pretty potent stuff. Now, she had two inches of the stuff in her cup. She did the same, downing the amber liquid in the hopes of feeling warmer. Immediately, she began choking on the Scotch again. "I better check on Burpy."

"Who?"

"Burpy, the dog." Jamaica disappeared into the next room with a piece of cheese. She returned without it. "He's okay. Ate the cheese but went back to sleep."

Ronnie nodded. Silence descended over the cramped back room. Ronnie took a piece of apple, snapping it in half with his teeth and chewing slowly, his eyes on Jamaica. Jamaica nibbled on the cheese and crackers, her eyes glancing all around the office area, taking in his work area.

The lights went off. The steady hum of the refrigerated cases and freezers stopped.

All was silent.

"Great," they said in unison.

Jamaica heard movement beside her. She hoped Ronnie was searching his desk for matches. Did he have a candle? She had some at her shop. Little good they did her there.

My shop. Crap. There goes all my ice cream, she thought. Instinctively she tried to look at her watch. Of course, she couldn't see it in the dark. She pulled out her cellphone, hit the button. It was dead. The swim in the water had destroyed it. Regardless, chances were the cellphone tower was also out of power. Which meant it would be a long while before they got power restored to the whole town.

A scraping sound followed by a spark and a flash of a match joined the smell of sulfur. Ronnie held the match aloft as he dug in the top drawer of his desk, searching for a candle. He found a candlestick, brought it out and tried to light it before burning his fingers with the match. The wick took the flame, sputtered a second, then flared to a normal flame. Ronnie looked for a place to set down the candle. "Here, hold this," he said, shoving the candle into Jamaica's hand. He rooted in a plastic bag near the back door and came up with a beer bottle. He took the empty beer bottle, stuffed the candlestick into the top until it held steady. On the desk, the candle threw light around a small perimeter of the desk, casting deep shadows beyond its reach.

"Guess this means we're in the thick of it now," Jamaica quipped.

"I doubt it. The eye is not supposed to arrive here until around three." Ronnie replied. He reached for another piece of cheese before settling in his chair. With nothing left to do but pout, Jamaica made herself comfortable on a box.

The storm winds continued to rage outside, howling and whistling through the cracks in the back door. The despondent sound got to Jamaica's nerves and combined with exhaustion and the Scotch, she started to tear up. Here was the one man she had loved for as long as she could remember, and there was so much emotional distance between them they could never overcome. A welling formed inside her, from the pit of her gut up her chest and into her throat. She began to cry and whimper along with the sound of the wind, unable to hold it back any longer.

Getting up from his chair, Ronnie put his arm around her shoulders. "Aw, come on Jam. It's not that bad." He patted her back. "Tell me what's wrong."

"Everything's wrong," she sniffled. "I can't stand it."

Ronnie kept trying to soothe her, rubbing his palm in circles over her upper back. "What's wrong?"

"You and me," she said. "Don't you ever wonder what would have happened or not happened if we had never gone to that party?"

Ronnie's hand stilled a moment before resuming its path. "We'd probably have gotten married and had a family, just like we talked about."

Jamaica burst into tears, crying harder this time. Through her tears she muttered, "But you had to go and take up with Brenda."

"Now, there's where you're wrong." Ronnie crouched down to kneel in front of Jamaica and look her in the eyes. "That night at the party. After our big fight. I left with Brenda. I don't deny that. She was too drunk to drive. I took her keys away and gave her a ride home. That was it, Jamaica, I swear it."

Jamaica blinked away her tears as she stared at him. "You mean, nothing happened?"

"That's exactly what I mean. Nothing happened. I would never take advantage of an intoxicated woman, you know that."

She had to nod in agreement. She did know that. And she was surprised the thought had never occurred to her in all these years. Brenda was drunk that night. Ronnie never would have had sex with someone who couldn't give full, sober consent.

"But afterwards, at school, you guys were always together," Jamaica said.

"She kept hounding me. She thought we should get together," Ronnie explained. "But I didn't want Brenda. All I wanted was you. If you recall, I tried to talk to you. You got mad and tried to sock me in the nose. Ended up on your ass instead."

"You were trying to apologize?"

He nodded before brushing her hair away from her face.

Bursting into tears again, Jamaica pitched forward and lay her head on Ronnie's shoulder.

"What are you crying for now?" Ronnie asked, his voice perplexed.

"All the time we missed being together," Jamaica wailed.

Ronnie pulled her closer and leaned his head against hers and let her cry.

When her tears finally subsided, Ronnie gently pushed Jamaica back to a sitting position. "My knees and thigh can't take this hardwood floor anymore." he said, as he gingerly stood and stretched his legs. He walked a couple of circles before he reached for the candle. "I'm going to the other room. Want to come with me or would you prefer sit here in the dark alone?" he asked.

"I'll go with you." Jamaica got up from her seat on a box.

Carrying the candle, Ronnie stopped at his desk. After searching through a drawer, he led her into the front room. As she followed, Jamaica admired his muscular silhouette. Her fingers itched to reach out and stroke his bare skin, to feel the rippling muscles and toned abs beneath her palms. Jamaica wasn't sure if it was the dimly lit space or the Scotch, but she felt lightheaded and dizzy just looking at Ronnie's naked torso.

It was eerily quiet without the motor on the freezer cases and refrigerated candy display case working. Burpy lay, still wet, in the corner, fast asleep.

Ronnie walked over to the ice cream freezers, set the candle on top of the sneeze shield shelf and reached for the scoop and a dessert cup. "Want some?" he asked. "It's going to all melt anyway."

"Sure, why not."

Ronnie gestured the length of the freezer with the scoop.

"How about a scoop of chocolate, one of coffee and a scoop of toffee crunch," she said after consulting the menu board with the list of flavors.

Ronnie scooped her order and then one for himself, cherry vanilla and raspberry swirl.

He added a flourish of whipped cream from a canister, and a maraschino cherry.

"Topping?"

"No thanks."

Leaning his back against the wall behind the ice cream freezer, Ronnie slid down it until he sat on the floor, legs stretched out before him.

Jamaica sat down in lotus beside him, her back against the wall.

They ate in silence. The ticking of a battery powered clock the only sound in the room.

Suddenly, Ronnie stuck his fingers in his raspberry swirl, leaned over and smeared it across Jamaica's cheek.

She jerked away at the coldness. "What the hell'd you do that for?" she sputtered.

"I wanted to see if it tasted better." He leaned over and swiped his tongue over the ice cream, lapping it up in one swoop. "It does. Let me try the other cheek." He turned her face, stuck his fingers in the cherry vanilla and smeared it across her cheek.

Jamaica, unsure about the first incident, now found the whole thing ridiculous. She laughed nervously as he leaned over and licked the ice cream off.

"Delicious." He sat back and looked at her. "You want to try it? I'll bet chocolate tastes great on me."

I'll bet it does too, but your cheek isn't what I want to lick it from. Jamaica face flushed hotly.

"Don't be bashful. Try it," Ronnie urged.

Jamaica picked up a small glob of chocolate ice cream and smeared it on Ronnie's left cheek. She leaned over and licked it off. The luscious, creamy texture was a sharp contrast to his scratchy five o'clock shadow. A shiver ran through her body and it was more than just the ice cream.

"Well, what do you think?" he asked, smirking. The scar above his left eyebrow rising as he smiled broadly.

"Not bad. Let me try the coffee, now."

She smeared the coffee ice cream across his right cheek, then licked. Her lady parts quivered.

"Not bad. But I like my coffee ice cream stronger."

"Touché,"

Jamaica ate her ice cream in silence.

Ronnie nudged her shoulder. "What about your toffee crunch?" he grinned even bigger.

"What about it?" Jamaica said, as she went on eating her ice cream with a spoon.

He winked. "Aren't you going to try it?"

"Where?" Jamaica asked. She gave him a devilish grin and a wink.

"I know." He took her cup, scooped a dollop of ice cream and smeared it across his lips.

"Don't be obvious or anything," Jamaica stared at him, salivating.

"Come on, Jam. It's cold." She didn't need any further encouragement.

Jamaica leaned over and licked the ice cream from his lips. In an instant, his lips parted and his tongue swirled out to meet hers.

Their kiss was sweet, gentle, and tentative. Ronnie leaned into their kiss, arms at his sides, bracing himself from falling. As it deepened, he rocked forward onto his knees, bringing Jamaica up onto her knees with him. His arms went around her to gather her close as she leaned into the kiss. It was unlike any kiss he'd ever experienced. Tender but assertive. Jamaica knew what she wanted and wasn't afraid to go for it. The thought surprised him and he moaned his appreciation.

After what seemed like a marathon kiss, he pulled away, tilting her head to the side, leaving her neck exposed for his next kiss. The middle of her shoulder looked too inviting to pass up. Ronnie's lips found the sensitive skin, leaving a trail of kisses from the starting point to her ear lobe. He nipped the lobe with his lips, before exploring all the curves and nuances of her ear with the tip of his tongue.

Jamaica gasped with each new advance. First her neck, next her ear. She tried not to moan too loudly but it was beyond her control. The sounds escaped no matter how hard she tried to control them. Memories of their one night together came flooding back to her. She shivered with the thought. Eyes closed, she let the sensations take over her.

Ronnie broke away, scooped a finger full of raspberry swirl from his cup. He smeared it on Jamaica's neck, then proceeded to lick it off, one long, sensuous lap at a time. Her gasp at the cold, runny ice cream was audible. If he hadn't been holding her with his left hand, she might have lunged away. But he held her in place, close enough to continue his ministrations.

She panted with the feel of his hot tongue on the cold skin where the ice cream was spread. The differences in temperature and the differences in texture making the action more alluring. She opened her eyes and watched as Ronnie brought another finger full of ice cream to her skin. This time, he smeared it on the exposed front of her neck. She gasped as it ran down her collarbone and onto her décolletage. A shiver ran down her chest as it hit. And again, as Ronnie's lips grazed the area, licking up the ice cream as they traveled. Jamaica couldn't stand it anymore. She wanted in on the action.

She pushed Ronnie away, and seized her own, melting cup of ice cream. Using two fingers, she scooped up some chocolate ice cream before taking his arm, spread it in a neat line from palm to inner elbow. Satisfied with the work, she began nibbling and licking her way, up from his palm to his wrist, up his forearm to his inner elbow. A hissing sound escaped his lips as she went, telling her he was enjoying the sensations as much as she did.

"Like that?" she whispered. Ronnie groaned in response. She slid her hands down his sides, and reached into her cup for more ice cream. A glob of coffee ice cream swirled into liquid on his chest. Jamaica went to work, licking and lapping at the well-defined pecs of his muscular chest. He cried out her name as her tongue glanced over his nipples, lapping at the ice cream swirled around them.

"Fair is fair." He reached for her shirt, grasped the ends, and pulled it over her head. Her lacy bra came off next as Ronnie proceeded to repeat his experience for Jamaica, giving her as good as he got.

She nearly burst into tears as he sucked at her ice cream-covered nipples, first the left, then the right. The feelings were so intense, so incredible, and so intimate, she could hardly stand them. As Ronnie had finished removing what he had smeared, Jamaica took his hand and pulled him to his feet with her as she stood. His brows craned together, his eyes showing his bewilderment. Until she reached for the waistband of his jeans. He helped her unbutton and unzip them, waiting as she slid them down his muscular legs and helped him step out of them.

    He was erect and expectant. Before tossing the pants aside he reached into a pocket. On her knees, she picked up a glob of toffee ice cream and smeared it on his maleness, immediately engulfing him with her lips to suck the cold ice cream off. Ronnie's hands went to her head, his fingers grasping her hair as she licked him clean. His breath was ragged as she made sure she got every drop of ice cream. Then she continued, searching lower for any drips and dribbles of melted cream along his balls. He gasped as she searched, his fingers tightening in her hair, pulling her head upward until she was standing before him.

    He looked into her eyes, tilted his head and smirked. Leaning over he kissed her deeply again, letting his tongue taste the ice cream she had just devoured. All the while, he reached for her panties, breaking the kiss only long enough to help her shimmy out of them. Freed of them, he skimmed his hands down her sides, from her breasts to her thighs. Jamaica's breath hitched then shuddered as he slipped his hand over her mound. She was hot and wet. Oh, so wet. Wetter than she had been their first time, on the couch in her shop.

    As he continued to stroke in the valley of her thighs, he kissed her hungrily. Her arms wound around his torso, pulling him closer. Insistently, she pulled him to her until there was no space, no light, no air between them. Melded together, they clung to each other, kissing so deeply Ronnie expected her to gasp for air. But she took all the tongue he offered, giving back when he tired of his probing.

    A bead of moisture formed on the tip of his hardness, a hardness that kept getting harder than it had ever been in his entire life. Here, now, he was with Jamaica. Unlike the last time when he was preoccupied with not wanting to hurt her. This time, he knew it would be better for her. And it would be better for him. He strained to control and contain himself, to not rush but it was damn near impossible.

Jamaica reached down as they kissed, grasping his erection. It throbbed in her hands. He could tell she wanted him. More so than she did the last time. Jamaica tried to push him onto his back. She wanted him lying down. The thought of her sinking down onto him and teasing him until they both could not stand it any longer was appealing. Reaching out, he snatched up the condom packet he had pulled out of his pants pocket earlier. He pressed it into the palm of her hand. When she realized what it was, she made haste applying it, rolling the thin membrane down his length.

His hands kneaded her body. Feeling her softness and substance. It excited him further to see her reaction, the widened eyes, the gasping, inarticulate noises from her throat. He sank his teeth into the column of her throat, reveling in the feel of her voice as it traveled through the skin and tendons beneath his lips. Damn her for stroking him so expertly. The motion, the feel of her soft hand on him.

His fingers sought out the source of the wetness between her thighs. They dipped into the well of nectar, she whimpered at his insertion, arching her back and shifting her hips forward to take more. He obliged, dipping deeper into the well, feeling the quivering of her muscles as he did so. She was ready. And he was too.

He lay her down on the floor, shifting his weight to his knees as he crawled between her own. Her sex, glistening with moisture, was open and ready for him. He pulled her closer, slid between her thighs and poised himself at her channel. Jamaica's hands pulled at him, at his waist and hips, trying to draw him into herself. He held back, waiting for her need to reach a fever pitch. He wanted to feel her explosion as soon as he entered her.

As her moaning and whimpering had reached a high, insistent pitch, he thrust deeply into her wetness. She cried out as she came. Ronnie could feel the convulsions of her muscles around himself. He leaned over and kissed her mouth, trailing a line of kisses down to her breasts. He cupped one breast, letting his thumb play and roll the hardened peak as he remained still inside her, feeling the contractions coming slower.

Jamaica tried to sit up. He nudged her back down. "On top," she breathed. "I want to be on top."

Ronnie acquiesced. He would give her the top position, hold out as long as he could, then flip her beneath him. He pulled her close, and rolled over, narrowly missing the side of the ice cream freezer.

Jamaica resettled herself upon his erection. She sank down, taking him in as much as she could, then rose up. Again, she sank down, going deeper this time. She continued this maneuver until she was impaled on his full length. Ronnie raised his hips with every dip of her bottom. Giving her every inch. She leaned over and nipped at his lips, the shift in her position grinding her hard button against his groin. Rocking gently, Ronnie felt the heat and sensations rising again inside her. Ronnie's hand grasped her hips, helping her, guiding her as she stroked against him. The rocking motions coalesced into a frenzied pitch. Driving herself forward one last time, striking hard on her button. As Ronnie watched, she came hard, exploding in every direction.

Ronnie hung on to her hips for his life. Teeth clenched, he knew he couldn't, knew he wouldn't last much longer if she continued with this motion. He sat up, grasped her by the waist, pulled her pelvis down to his own and rolled her onto her back, giving him the upper advantage.

He nestled closer between her thighs, letting his free hand skim her breast, tweaking the nipple as it passed. She moaned aloud again, clearly experiencing another mounting of sensations. He stroked into her slowly, reveling in the wetness, the firmness, the velvety softness of her. Teeth clenched, he did it again, and again, holding back on the urge to abandon this slow pace and pound into her. He wanted her to come with him, to feel the convulsions of her channel as he spilled himself into her sweetness.

Her breathing hitched. Her moaning came loud and unending. Her hands reached out for him. He kept it slow, had to keep it slow until the best possible moment.

That moment came when she called out his name, her velvet sheath pulsing around him. He could not wait any longer. He thrust into her once, then faster and furiously made her his own. He surged forward with one last push before spilling into her. Collapsing on top of her, he joined her in moaning out his pleasure.

They remained wrapped in each other's arms for a few minutes, enjoying the aftermath of their desire. His head resting on her chest, listening to her racing heartbeat slow to a more normal rate.

"This floor is getting cold." She poked him in the side with her finger, "Get up, please."

He got up, coming into a lotus position on the floor, surrounded by their discarded clothing.

"Yeah, I got that too." Helping her to sit up, he handed over the shirt, then watched as she put it on. She leaned over on all fours and searched out her panties. Ronnie reached out for his jeans, as she scrambled on the floor looking for them. Clothing sorted, they finished dressing in silence. The only sounds being the ticking of the clock and the howling of the hurricane outside.

Ronnie stood and walked over to the front window. "Looks like it's letting up a little."

"Thank God," she said. "I hope everything is okay at my shop. Well, besides there not being any power, anyway." She walked over and stood beside him, looking outside the window at Main Street. Jamaica placed her hand on the small of Ronnie's back and rubbed lightly, trying to keep contact. Since Ronnie didn't respond, she dropped her hand. *So much for maintaining the afterglow.*

The street was one gigantic river. The storm drains must have been stopped up with leaves and debris. Even if they hadn't, they never could keep up with the amount of water running down the street. Rain came down in sheets, sideways. At times, it even appeared to be raining upwards, back toward heaven. There wasn't any lightning or thunder to break up the monotonous nature of the deluge.

Ronnie put his arm around Jamaica's shoulders, pulling her to him. Surprised at his touch, she pulled away slightly at first, then let him hug her, and gave in to the feeling, putting her head against his shoulder and snuggling there. He turned toward her, taking her completely in his arms. "You know how much I've missed you all these years?" he dropped a kiss on her forehead.

"No. If it's as much as I missed you, it's a lot."

"Whatever are we going to do, Jam?"

They stood in silence, holding each other, watching the destruction outside.

"I can't speak for you, but I'll still be here at this shop. And I hope you'll continue here somehow," he said gazing into his eyes.

"I hope so too." Dropping her head on his shoulder, she muttered, "I don't know how."

"What are your options?" He still held her to his chest, his arms around her waist.

"Well, I'd like a bakery. You know, with everything from bread to pastry and cakes."

"That sounds great. Why not?"

Jamaica decided to lay it all out on the table. "Well, to be blunt, it takes a lot of capital investment for ovens, mixers, and display cases for that kind of operation. It's not going to be cheap."

In her mind's eye, Jamaica could see the rows of pastries, baskets of different kinds of breads. It would be colorful and smell oh so wonderful.

"Any other options?" he asked.

"I was thinking coffee shop. Like fancy coffees. Lattes, cappuccinos, and espresso. All that kind of stuff. It's less of an investment since I would have the tables and chairs and stuff."

They looked out the window as the wind seemed to die down, and the rain slackened, each in their own thoughts.

"And both? Could you do both? Maybe start with coffees and the small baked goods and add breads and cakes as the business grows?" Ronnie asked, turning into their embrace.

"I suppose I could do that. Grow the business up." Jamaica's eyes brightened a bit and she smiled.

"That sounds the most appealing to me." Ronnie offered. "And you can decide what you want to add and when."

Silence continued as they were each lost in the visions of Jamaica's store as it might be in the future. A fancy espresso machine, a barista behind the counter, fresh baked goodies in the display case to go along with the coffees.

"I think it's a brilliant idea," Ronnie encouraged, his voice upbeat.

"I hope so. I've put everything I own into my store. I have to turn it into something to support myself. I can't lose it now."

He took her hand, and stroked the back of it with his thumb. "I'm sorry, you know. Sorry you have to start over."

"We made a deal...a bet really. I lost. This town can't support two ice cream parlors."

"I wish we could have figured out something else."

She cocked her head aside. "I was too blindsided and too stubborn to see or consider any other options." She snuggled closer to him as they looked out the window together. "I only hope I can transform my shop into something this town will embrace."

"Don't worry, the people of this town will support you in whatever avenue you choose." He kissed her temple. "Now, what about us?" he asked, giving her a little squeeze. "What's to happen with us?"

Jamaica turned to look him square in the eyes. "I don't know, Ronnie. What do you want to happen?"

"I still love you, Jam. I never stopped. Despite all the years and the distance. I've never stopped loving you."

A smile broke out on Jamaica's face. "I know the feeling. I never stopped loving you either. God knows I tried."

Ronnie's eyes bore into Jamaica's. "I'm sorry I was such a jerk back then. But I've changed. I have to say, I want us together again. Nothing would be better than living each day with you in it,"

"Me neither."

"So, what do we do? Continue working across the street from each other?" He stared into her eyes, hope and eagerness smoldering in them.

"It's a start." Jamaica smiled and planted a ravenous kiss on his lips. "It would be a big help if you stopped associating with Brenda Tardash."

"Consider it done. Seriously. I asked her to leave the other day. Told her not to come back, ever." He shook his head. "I should never have accepted her offer of help at the festival. I just encouraged her to expect more."

"Why did you?"

"Desperation. I didn't know who to ask. I needed help and she offered. I couldn't say no."

She looked in his eyes. "Do you know, the morning after we slept together, she came to tell me you two were an item?"

The shock on Ronnie's face made it clear to her it was genuine. "Seriously?"

"And I saw her give you a kiss at your shop door. That's why I was so pissed at you."

He sighed, his chin hanging to his chest. "That's why. Makes sense now." He turned to face her. "Brenda is out of my life for good. It's only you I love, Jamaica."

"Thanks." Jamaica leaned into him for another hug.

He chuckled. "Oh, I didn't do it for you. She was driving me crazy. She seemed to think we were going to pick up where we left off from high school." Ronnie hugged Jamaica closer, then let her go.

"I don't find that at all surprising."

"She was hinting that since she helped me out so much at the festival, maybe I should make her my assistant manager. Can you imagine?" He stepped away, walking to the middle of the store floor. "Well, I don't have to worry about her anymore. She ran out of here like a rat off a burning ship."

Jamaica giggled, an image of Brenda fleeing the scene vivid in her mind.

Ronnie took her hand and pulled gently. "Come on. I'm hungry. Do we have any more cheese and pepperoni left?"

"Only you could think of your stomach at a time like this."

"There isn't much else to do, unless you're ready for round two?"

Jamaica took off running for the back room. "Maybe I am!"

CHAPTER TWENTY-THREE

Early the next morning, Jamaica and Ronnie joined the crowds of people picking their way along Main Street. By then, the water had receded to the Fulton River's swollen banks. But the streets remained impassable. Besides a thick layer of mud, they were littered with a wide assortment of debris: building materials, dead animals, propane tanks, patio furniture, dumpsters, logs, brush, and overturned vehicles.

The water had breached the lower sidewalk on Jamaica's side of the street. All the stores on the west side of Main Street were flooded during the height of the storm while the east side remained above the water line.

The front window pane of Jamaica's shop had shattered allowing the water to penetrate inside. The floor was coated with a thick layer of mud, as were the tables and chairs. All those white tables and chairs were scattered about, most overturned and dark brown with a coating of mud. The freezer cases were also damaged, their motors having been submerged during the flood.

Even the kitchen suffered, though not as bad. The stainless-steel worktables and the industrial gas stove's tall legs kept them out of the water's reach. Jamaica thought the couch had survived until she noticed the soaked cushions. The dank smell of early mold was already beginning to form.

Everyone began cleaning as best they could without power or clean water. It took seven days for the power to be restored. Both Jamaica and Ronnie had cleaned out their ice cream freezers and refrigerators. Rather than let the masses of ice cream melt completely and make a mess, they spent the entire night emptying the freezers. The contents went directly into the nearest remaining upright dumpster. Within hours, a river of multi-colored cream was seen dripping from the metal dumpster into the nearest storm drain.

Jamaica thanked God she had the foresight to continue paying her business insurance despite losing the contest. It took a while, but the insurance adjuster finally showed up to declare the contents of the shop a total loss. At the most crucial time, the store had serendipitously provided Jamaica with the funds to re-vamp her business into a new venture.

Ronnie's store survived relatively unscathed minus the ice cream and candy having to be destroyed. He also had business insurance that covered the loss of food products and income while the store remained closed.

Empire Kitchens Ice Creams was not disturbed by Hurricane Mindy. They were back in production, and worked around the clock, to make up for the lost time and revenue while they were shut down for disinfection. In increments, ice cream was delivered to Ronnie's store. Within two months, he had restored his stock.

Some store owners didn't fare so well.

Kevin poked his head around the archway into the kitchen one morning when Jamaica was taking inventory of the remaining, useable cooking and baking utensils.

He looked downcast, like he'd lost his best friend. Jamaica set down her pad and pen on the stainless-steel table and walked over to greet him.

"Kevin, what's wrong." It was a rhetorical question. These days, there was so much still wrong. The power was back on, as was the water service. It was a tremendous help with the clean-up but there was still much to do, it was overwhelming for every merchant in town, as well as the affected homeowners.

"Hey, Jamaica. I wanted to tell you the news," Kevin said in a quiet voice, his hands folded over his stomach as though holding in his emotions.

"What, Kevin? Is it bad?" Jamaica's eyes darted over his face. She reached out and put her arms around him. "What's happened?"

His shoulders slumped under her arms. "Maddie and I talked it over and we decided it's time to close the shop."

"Oh, Kevin, that's terrible news! What are you going to do?" Jamaica gave him a squeeze.

"Not sure yet. I didn't have insurance. And we don't have the capital to rebuild the business." Like Jamaica's store, the windows had blown in, allowing his store to be hit hard with flood water. He had lost everything, including thousands of dollars of inventory. Without business insurance, there was no way to recoup his loses.

Two days later, Kevin came back one last time to say goodbye.

"What're you goin' to do now, Jam?" Kevin asked, arms outstretched to give Jamaica a big hug.

Jamaica sat on her heels and stopped washing the stove to talk. She stood and slipped off her rubber gloves. "I'm thinking of a bakery. I have the money now. And I've always wanted to own a bakery." She walked into his arms and hugged him close.

"It's a great idea. There isn't one for twenty miles."

Jamaica pulled back to look him in the face. "We'll see how it works out," she said, her face illuminated by her smile.

It took several trips to the local bank but they were fruitful trips. Within two months Jamaica had secured the extra capital needed to build her dream. A flurry of equipment buying and the hiring of a bakery assistant with considerable experience ensued.

CHAPTER TWENTY-FOUR

"And with the cutting of this ribbon, we present to you, the newest addition to downtown Fulton River, Jam Bakery!" Mayor Marguerite D'Anguerra turned to Jamaica, giving her a nod.

A flash of sunlight reflected off the scissors in her trembling hand as Jamaica cut the wide red satin ribbon stretched across the storefront of her new bakery. The crowd roared and clapped then surged forward toward the open door. A few people stopped to congratulate Jamaica, most notably her father and Mary.

Ronnie materialized beside her and planted a kiss on her cheek. "Congratulations sweetheart."

She flung her arms around him, giving him a huge hug. "Thank you. Thank you for all your help getting the shop ready, and all your support." The sound of laughter inside the shop drew their attention to the throng inside. "I better check to see if I can help them with anything."

She stepped inside the doorway and paused as she had so many times in the last weeks. The sales and eating area of the bakery took up the area formerly occupied by Kevin's Card and Gift Store. The Emporium space had become mostly the bakery's kitchen and a small portion was now the sales counter. The black and white tiled flooring remained as did the table and chairs from the emporium, at least for now. The marble counter from the ice cream shop had been shortened and two six-foot display cases replaced the ice cream freezers.

Behind the counter, along the back wall, Jamaica had tiled the wall with a harlequin pattern on which shelving hung with baskets of fresh bread, buns, and bagels. A bright red awning hanging over the sales area and sunshine yellow walls gave the interior of her new shop a vibrant, cheerful, and playful appearance. And the smells coming from the cases and kitchen filled the entire space with sweet aromas of bread, sugar, chocolate, and coffee.

Cutting a path through the mob wasn't easy. When she got behind the sales counter, she asked Jackie Thorndike if she needed anything.

The petite brunette replied, "If you're offering another pair of hands, that would be wonderful."

Jamaica donned an apron and started filling orders. The crowd thinned within half an hour. Pleased with how well the team had worked together, Jamaica called a huddle. "Thank you all for all your expert help. Everything went so smoothly, I hardly feel necessary. And that's a good thing!"

Turning to Jackie, her baking assistant, "All of the baked goods, the breads, cookies, brownies, pastries, everything looked amazing, Jackie. I am so glad to have found and hired you!" Jamaica held out her hand.

"You mean you're so glad you were able to steal her from that bakery in Boston!" One of the sales clerks laughed.

Jamaica nodded fiercely as a blush spread across Jackie's face. "I'm so glad you hired me too. I love being back home in Vermont. And I love working here." She raised her glass of water, "Here's to Jamaica Jones and Jam Bakery!"

"To Jamaica Jones and Jam Bakery!"

Life was hectic for Jamaica, probably more so than when she ran the ice cream shop alone. Even with Jackie Thorndike beginning at two in the morning to start the bread and pastry doughs, Jamaica was in the bakery at four in the morning to help make the breakfast pastries and menu items. At six o'clock, the bakery opened for business, smelling like all kinds of sweetness. By six-thirty, she was in her father's kitchen, making his breakfast, before returning to the bakery for another couple of work hours.

As Ronnie had predicted, the response from the people in town was overwhelming. Jam Bakery quickly became a popular hangout.

Closing at three in the afternoon, Jamaica was free to visit Ronnie every day. They were, according to the local newspaper, an official item. After a brief awkward period, after the storm, they settled back into the loving relationship they had in high school. Ronnie spent many nights at Jamaica's apartment, which was bigger and closer to the center of town than his own studio apartment.

Ronnie's store continued to do well. With Jamaica's foresight and suggestion, he put together gift baskets for the holidays, selling out in a week. The steady cash flow meant he could hire an assistant manager. Kevin Dailey, freed from his own store, applied and was immediately accepted for the job. The two men got along well, complementing each other's strengths, and both being good with customers.

Which was how Jamaica Jones and Ronnie Caswell got a chance to have their first vacation in years, ending up in Las Vegas the last weekend of March at the annual Retail Confectioners International conference.

They entered the exhibit hall and stopped in their tracks. The program had said the exhibit hall was over one million square feet and had more than eighty-six vendor booths. The size didn't sink in until they saw the expanse.

"This is so overwhelming," Jamaica said, her eyes taking in the rows of booths. "I thought the educational sessions were amazing. Look at all this! Where should we start?" Jamaica asked Ronnie, looking down at the exhibit hall map. Indeed, she had been overwhelmed by the mass of information available to them for the last three days. There were over thirty different seminars available to them. So many, they had decided to split up to cover as many of them as they could. Later, over lunch or dinner, they would briefly share the information they had gathered at the assorted lectures.

Thus far, Ronnie had attended "Allergen Awareness," "Hiring the Right People," "What's Hot, What's Not," and "Merchandising Essentials." The last session on merchandising essentials was his favorite so far as it showed him how to build a brand image, create effective promotions, and assemble product displays and gift baskets. He was signed up for three additional sessions: "Soft Serve and Hard Scoop

Novelties," "Setup and Manage Your Own Website," and "Understanding Chocolate."

While there was little pertaining directly to Jamaica's bakery business, she did enjoy "Understanding the Food Safety Modernization Act," "Customer Service," and "Upselling for Profits." She was also signed up for upcoming lectures on "Payroll for Dumbbells" and "Essentials of Flavor Combinations." Tomorrow afternoon they were both planning to attend a session called "Flavor Trends."

They stood near the entry way watching the swarm of confectioners stream toward the booths. "I don't know how you do this. Let's start left to right, front to back until we're seen them all," Ronnie said.

"Don't forget we each have sessions at one o'clock. And we need to eat."

"Well, from the looks of the free samples being offered at these booths, I'd say we won't have to worry about lunch, unless you want something more nutritious than candy."

"I think I can handle candy for one day." Jamaica smiled and they headed off down the first row of booths. By the end of the next hour, they had only visited a quarter of the booths. It was clear they were going to have to return after their sessions to get through a few more booths and spend more time in the exhibit hall tomorrow between sessions.

"Maybe we should have a look at the list of vendors and decide if there are any in particular we definitely want to get to before the exhibit hall closes tomorrow night," Ronnie suggested.

"Yeah, that's a great idea. We also could split up again, like we are for the lecture sessions."

"I don't want to be in Las Vegas without you by my side." Ronnie took Jamaica's arm in his as they walked out of the exhibit hall on the way to the session rooms.

MELT MY HEART

Later that night, after dinner at the famed Caravello Ristorante at the Venetian Casino, they stepped outside on the balcony of their hotel room, thirty-six stories up, for some fresh air. Below them, the lights of the city were ablaze though it had just barely turned to dusk. As far as the eye could see, the lights stretched out before them to the perimeter of the city, where the desert disappeared into darkness.

They stood side by side at the railing, watching the glitter and glamour of the lights, the fountain of the Bellagio Hotel, the Pirate Ship at the Treasure's Hotel. For the first time that day, silence descended between them. It had been a long, hard, active day. So much information was thrown at them in the three-hour sessions. It was hard to keep up writing notes, let alone asking questions without seeming like a total hick.

"Excuse me a second," Ronnie said, before disappearing into the hotel room.

He was back in a few minutes. Jamaica was engrossed watching a traffic accident unfold a block away on the strip. Out of the corner of her eye, she saw Ronnie come up beside her, then seem to bend over.

"What happened?" she gasped, reaching to help him up.

"I fell in love." Ronnie got down on one knee. "I fell in love with you in high school and I never stopped loving you. Despite all the years, despite all the distance between us."

Jamaica was speechless as she watched Ronnie reach into his pocket and pull out a ring.

He continued, "I know this is sudden, but I'm sure of the way I feel and I'm pretty sure you feel the same way."

Jamaica stared at the diamond solitaire ring held between Ronnie's thumb and index finger.

"Jamaica Jones, will you be my wife?" he asked, his voice cracking.

"Oh, Ronnie! Oh my God! Of course, I will."

Ronnie took her left hand and slid the ring on to her finger. She held it out to admire the beauty and sparkle of it in the lights of the city around them.

"Let's get married now. While we're here in Vegas." Taking her hand in his and stroking the back of it, he waited for her response.

"Here? Now? Ronnie, I couldn't do that to my Dad. He'd be heartbroken if he missed my wedding." Her eyes filling with unshed tears, her lips quivered.

"Okay, let's get married here, secretly, this weekend. And then have another service, like a church wedding, with your Dad and all our friends invited. We won't tell them we've already done the deed beforehand." Ronnie squeezed both her hands. "Jam, I can't wait. Let's do it now. Tonight, in fact."

"Tonight?" Jamaica's voice hitched up an octave. "What will I wear?"

"Wear what you're wearing now. You can have a real wedding dress for the church wedding," he suggested.

Jamaica was silent a few minutes, staring out over the city. Her right hand playing with the ring on her left hand.

"Okay Ronnie, I don't want to wait another day either." She smiled, wiping her eyes. "Let's do it!"

CHAPTER TWENTY-FIVE

FULTON RIVER GAZETTE
Local Enemies Kiss and Make Vows

Two of Fulton River's own have tied the knot after a summer of friction. Jamaica Jones, former owner of the Vermont Ice Cream Emporium and Ronald Caswell, owner of the Fulton's Creamery and Confections joined in wedded bliss on April 30th. Father Michael at St. Brigid Church officiated at the candlelight event.

Mrs. Jones-Caswell wore a gorgeous white satin sheath gown with a crepe-back, a plunging neckline and a pearl and bead encrusted edge, created by Vera Wang. A bouquet of white roses from Regina Maxwell's shop, Gina Blooms, finished the look as she walked down the aisle on her father, Mr. Sydney Jones' arm.

Mr. Caswell dressed in an Italian cut black tuxedo with notched labels, a white shirt, and a black bow tie. A simple white rosebud boutonniere adorned his jacket.

Readers might remember Ms. Jones and Mr. Caswell went head-to-head in an ice cream war at the Fulton River Festival back in August. The contest winner, Mr. Caswell, won "Best Ice Cream in Fulton River" while the losing store owner, Ms. Jones, had to close up shop. She has since expanded and reopened her storefront as Jam Bakery.

Several other Fulton River shops participated in the nuptial arrangements. Madelaine Dailey of Dailey Photography served as photographer for the event. And Jackie Thorndike, Mrs. Jones-Caswell's assistant at Jam Bakery made the wedding cake and oversaw the preparation of the reception foods.

After the evening ceremony, the happy couple and small contingent of guests assembled at Jam Bakery for wedding cake, ice cream, hors d'oeuvres and cocktails.

When asked about their honeymoon, Mr. Caswell and Mrs. Jones-Caswell said they recently were in Las Vegas for a convention, and it was sort of like a honeymoon. At least for now. They would take a real honeymoon, in a few weeks' time, to someplace warm, like Jamaica, of course.

THE END

Melt My Heart Bonus Recipes
Jamaica's Hot Fudge Sauce
2/3 cup heavy cream
¾ cup dark brown sugar, firmly packed
2 ounces unsweetened chocolate, chopped
1 ounce bittersweet chocolate chips
1 teaspoon vanilla
1 tablespoons unsalted butter
2 tablespoons light corn syrup
Using a heavy saucepan, heat t
1 teaspoon prepared dark roast coffee
1/8 teaspoon salt

Combine the heavy cream and sugar over medium heat until sugar is dissolved, stirring occasionally. Add chocolates, butter, and corn syrup, cooking and stirring just until smooth. Bring the mixture to a boil, then add coffee, and salt. Remove from heat and add vanilla. Serve hot over ice cream.

Emporium Butterscotch Sauce
1 cup light brown sugar, firmly packed
¼ cup light corn syrup
½ stick unsalted butter
Pinch, salt
½ cup heavy cream
1 teaspoon vanilla

Using a heavy saucepan, combine first four ingredients and cook over medium heat, stirring constantly until the sugar is dissolved. Boil the syrup WITHOUT Stirring, until candy thermometer registers 280^0F. Remove pan from heat and stir in heavy cream and vanilla, stirring until smooth. As it cools, sauce will thicken. Serve warm over ice cream.

Acknowledgments

I am grateful to the All-mighty for the blessing of a vivid imagination he bestowed on me since I was a little girl.

Honing that imagination into a story takes a lot of help. I am indebted to my critique partner, Valerie Lynne, for all her help whipping the early manuscript into something worthy of publishing. Thanks to my beta readers for pointing out some sticky spots. A huge thank you to my editor, Lynne Pearson of All That Editing LLC, for taking on this new author and helping her transform this work in ways I could not imagine! I am so grateful to be working with you!

I would be remiss if I failed to mention the awesome group of people in CTRWA, past and present, who have helped me learn the craft and art of writing romance and everything else that goes along with it like marketing, designing websites, book covers ,etc. Your help and camaraderie has been a highlight of my life.

A thank you shout out to the amazing Mel Jolly! In a nutshell, you taught me how to get my act together. I will forever be grateful for your words of wisdom and encouragement.

A very long time ago, my high school year book senior profile listed my ambition in life as " To be a writer". While it may never pay most of the bills it generates getting it to publishing stage, I can honestly say I did it!

DIANA ROCK

<u>More Books by Diana Rock</u>
<u>Fulton River Falls Series</u>
Melt My Heart
Proof of Love
Bloomin' In Love
First Christmas Ornament
Book #5- TBA (Release date 2023)

<u>Colby County Series</u>
Bid to Love
Courting Choices (Release date 10/8/2022)
Book #3 -TBA (Release date 2023)

<u>MovieStuds Series</u>
Hollywood Hotshot
Hollywood Hotdog (Release date 2023)

MELT MY HEART

BONUS MATERIAL

PROOF OF LOVE
Fulton River Falls Series: Book Two

Jackie Thorndike thought it was a nice thing to do before she left for the day. One last task before she finished today's shift at Jam Bakery. Steadying the tray as she walked, the heavy glass pitcher of lemonade and two glasses clanged together. Jackie put her back to the swinging kitchen door and gently pushed, entering the sales, and eating area of the bakery, where her boss, Jamaica Jones, and the new applicant were sitting.

Since they were seated around the corner in the farthest area of the bakery, Jackie had to walk past the display cases, now nearly empty of breakfast pastries and sweets. After closing time, they would not be restocked until five the next morning. Behind the display cases, in front of the harlequin-pattern tiled walls were baskets for breads, also empty. The overhanging awning of lipstick red, along with the sunshine yellow painted walls of the bakery made the place bright and cheerful. Far more cheerful than the windowless gray and steel of the commercial kitchen where she worked her entire shift.

Rounding the corner of the eating area, Jackie caught sight of her boss and the back of applicant. Jamaica sat uncomfortably at the café table. Across from her, the new applicant sat stiffly, his forearms resting on the tabletop, his back rigid. When she was within ten feet of them the man turned his head slightly to look out the window they sat beside.

Jackie Thorndike stopped abruptly in her tracks. She knew that profile. She knew that man. Swearing under her breath, she tried to decide whether to retreat to the kitchen before she was noticed or continue on with the refreshments. The last person she wanted to see applying for the open position was Mark Zutka and yet, here he was doing just that.

Before she could decide, Jamaica noticed her. "Ah, Jackie. Aren't you sweet, bringing us something to drink."

Mark Zutka looked over. His left eyebrow raised slightly, and a glimmer of a grin grew on his face. Even his eyes seemed to twinkle with laughter at her predicament. He folded his hands across his chest and smirked that stupid smirk she had always hated. That smirk always wanted to wipe off his face with the palm of her hand or a baseball bat.

Caught, she had no choice but to continue to the café table with the tray. The glasses clanged again as she approached. "I thought you might like some refreshment before I left for the day," she said, easing the tray down to table level.

Jackie saw Mark's hand reached out for one of the glasses. Before she could utter a word of warning, he lifted the glass, unbalancing the tray. The tray tilted back toward Jackie. She tried to reposition her hands, but it was too late. The pitcher tilted, spilling lemonade down the front of her shirt and pants. The cold wetness made her muscles stiffen as the liquid quickly soaked through her thin shirt and ran down her abdomen into her pants. Unable to move for fear of dropping the tray of glass, she stood shivering, silently feeling rivulets of the beverage ran down her legs, pooling on the floor.

Don't miss out!

Visit the website below and you can sign up to receive emails whenever Diana Rock publishes a new book. There's no charge and no obligation.

https://books2read.com/r/B-A-YUKN-BANMB

BOOKS 2 READ

Connecting independent readers to independent writers.

About the Author

Diana lives in eastern Connecticut with her tall, dark and handsome hero and one spoiled elderly kitty. She works full time as a histotechnologist, writing in her spare time. Diana likes puttering about the yard, baking and cooking, hiking, fly-fishing, and Scottish Country Dancing. Follow her exploits on her website, in her blogs and newsletters.

Read more at DianaRock.com.

CPSIA information can be obtained
at www.ICGtesting.com
Printed in the USA
BVHW032010090922
646320BV00006B/23